The World of the Forgotten
Lost Memories

Lunar Rose

Copyright © 2022 Lunar Rose

All rights reserved. No part of this book may be reproduced or transmitted in any form or by any means, electronic or mechanical, including photocopying, recording or by any information storage and retrieval system without permission in writing from the publisher.

Kyarra Raven—Mililani, HI
ISBN: 979-8-218-02506-9
Title: The World of the Forgotten: Lost Memories
Author: Lunar Rose
Digital distribution | 2022
Paperback | 2022

This is a work of fiction. The characters, names, incidents, places, and dialogue are products of the author's imagination, and are not to be construed as real.

Chapter 1

Descended of wizards,
Child of a god,
Favored by the wise,
A journey with solutions you must devise.
When seven keys shall be made one,
A door to another will be undone;
A mystical land is what will be found.
Forthwith a world in chains shall be unbound.

Noelani woke up startled. She looked around wondering where the voice came from and groaned when the sun shined in her eyes. She got up and closed the curtains. They were white but she had decorated them. On the left side a large beautiful, majestic black dragon whose scales sparkled like the night sky. On the right, another dragon with multi-colored scales starting at blue, fading through green and into brown with the tip of its tail being red. The dark green scales were decorated with flowers and the blue were decorated with clouds.

She turned around and looked at the mess of her small room. Except it was only messy in the sense that she had paper drawings everywhere there wasn't a single open space on the walls or ceiling. Even the door was covered front and back. Each and every drawing was a mythical creature of some sort, be it, god or monster, drawn how she imagines them.

With a soft sigh she got ready for school. The rest of the apartment wasn't much bigger than her room but it felt large and empty now that her older brother had moved off to college.

"Has Hunter called yet?" She asked her mom as she helped finish making breakfast.

"No, not yet," her mother said sadly.

"He's just busy mom, he hasn't forgotten about us."

"I know I just miss my baby boy."

"I miss him too."

Noelani's mom kissed her head then they both sat on the couch and ate. When they were done her mom drove her to school. She then went straight to the auditorium, sat in the back row, and watched some of the other student's audition for a school play. Before long, another girl comes up and sits next to her; "Hey, Lani. Watching Jake again?"

"No Rose. I'm watching the auditions, not just Jake," Noelani said, watching the said boy on the stage.

"You do know he's a jerk. Right?" Rose asked.

"Well, I don't think he is. I think it's an act," Noelani replied.

"Oh, so you think since he's the best male actor in the school he's acting like a jerk?"

"Yes."

"He is a bully. He made fun of you being poor last week."

"He only said that because his dumb girlfriend was there and she was already making fun of my clothes. Now she's just straight up mean."

"You are delusional."

"Hey, I see the good in people. Well, most people. Did you bring the books I wanted?"

"Nope, The Capital City Library didn't have them. "

Noelani sighed and opened her bag. She pulled out four books and handed them to Rose. "You can take these back now."

"You're getting faster. Usually I have to renew them before you finish."

Noelani shrugged. "I skipped my homework."

"You shouldn't do that. You could have asked me for help."

"I might just drop out already."

Rose gently smacked her arm.

"Ow! Hey!"

"You are not dropping out! You can't go to a good arts college if you drop out. Take out your homework, I'm helping you."

"Alright alright fine," Noelani groaned and opened her binder. "But you can't be there to help me pass the SAT's and I need to pass that on my own and my math is horrible."

"Hey what's this?" Rose pointed at a piece of paper where Neolani had written the words, she heard that morning.

"I don't know, I heard it in my dream. I thought if I could write it out, I'd figure it out. Thinking maybe it was a prophecy I read in one of the mythology books but it's not ringing any bells."

"Well let's not focus on it."

"Yeah ok," Nolani pulled out her homework and they worked on it together until classes started.

When it came to school; Noelani hates everything except Art, Music, Dance and Home EC. The only good thing that came from her father was the funding to go to a school with these classes. Unfortunately, he wouldn't fund anything else which made things hard. What she felt sucked the most was her favorite classes were after lunch.

Which was now. She leaned against the wall outside Rose's class waiting for her to come out but she was talking to Nate, her crush and it was taking longer than usual. As someone walked past her, they stuck a piece of paper in her hand and continued walking. She looked at the paper and it read: "Meet me in the library, your favorite section."

Her favorite section wasn't hard to find. It was the section with all the cat books because the school had very little when it came to mythology. She looked around but no one was there so she looked to see if there were any new cat books she could borrow. Suddenly someone decided to sneak up on her and tickle her sides, almost making her scream. Then the person covered her mouth. "Shhh,"

She turned around and pushed him away from her. "That was your fault, you jerk," she hissed in a low tone.

The boy chuckled and removed the hood of his Jacket. It was Jake the boy from the auditorium. "You're just too easy," he grinned as he adjusted his baseball hat backwards.

"You know we don't have to be sneaking around like this just so I can taste your homework," Noelani said grabbing the hat and putting it on his head the right way.

"Please. If my friends find out I like baking just as much as I like basketball and acting, they'd disown me. Besides, my girlfriend hates you."

"Get a new girlfriend and better friends. Simple as that."

"Hey, it's your birthday, right?" he asked, slipping his bag off his back obviously changing the subject.

"How did you know that?"

"I heard Rose talking about it a week ago." He took out a container and handed it to her.

Noelani opened it and found a single chocolate cupcake with a raspberry on top. "I made it with you in mind, you like raspberries, right?"

"Jake you—"

"Lani? Where are you?" Rose's voice came from nearby. Interrupting Noelani.

"Did you tell her I was here?"

"No. Of course not."

Jake put his hood back on and left quickly.

"Jeez," Noelani sighed and put the cupcake away.

"There you are," Rose said after finally finding her. "I thought you were going to wait for me?"

"I was. You were taking too long with Nate and I got bored."

"Well come on let's have lunch." Rose took her hand and gently pulled her to the cafeteria. "You might have to find a new library. One that'll actually let you in," she said as they ate.

"I'll start looking after school."

"How about after you finish your homework?"

"How about I try my homework for a few hours and then I'll look."

"Two hours of each subject that you hate," Rose bargained.

Noelani groaned. "Fine but can we go to the ice cream shop before you walk me home?"

"Duh. We always go to the Ice cream shop on your birthday."

"Thank you," Noelani said, relived that she can put off her homework as much as she can.

"Can I bring Nate with me?" Rose asked.

"Doesn't he have soccer after school?"

"Yeah, but he'll skip if I ask him too."

"Well this is your first crush and I don't want to get in the way of any spark that may be there so yeah he can come."

"YAY!" Rose beamed. Which made Noelani smile.

Chapter 2

After school they spent hours at the ice cream shop like they always do for her birthday. Despite Rose and Nate acting all lovey dovey and goofy, they made sure that Noelani didn't feel like a third wheel since it was her birthday. Then they walked Noelani home and watching the two new love birds made her happy. Unfortunately the happy faded when she walked into her house, with her mom still at work it was dark and empty. She spent two annoying headache inducing hours on her math.

Then her mom came home with dinner. Noelani's favorite Chinese meal and a cake. They celebrated her birthday a little more. She got new art stuff as a present and then they watched a couple movies before her mom went to bed and she went to her room to continue her homework. Around two in the morning she was just about to throw her science book across the room when there was a quiet knock on her window.

Deciding it was best not to throw the book since they didn't have the money to pay for any damages, she set it down next to her then opened her curtain to find Jake. Confused, she left her room and the house. "What are you doing here?" she asked as she walked to him.

"I need to know how it tasted. Your birthday present was also this week's Home EC homework."

"You could have stayed and found out when you gave it to me."

"If Rosaline saw me, she would have given me trouble."

"That's because she thinks you are a jerk. If you just let her see this side of you, she'll change her mind."

"I doubt that," Jake said stubbornly.

Noelani rubbed her head, her headache was getting worse. "I haven't tried it yet. Come inside my room is the first door on the right."

"Cool thanks." He followed her inside. "Your place is small," he said in surprise.

"Really? I hadn't noticed," she said sarcastically, as she made a glass of water and grabbed some ibuprofen.

"How can you afford going to our school?"

"Dad. He's some sort of 'actor' though I've never seen any of his work. Anyway because of that he wants his kids to be in the arts as well. That's the only money he spends on us. My brother used to tell me that dad always said, 'If it has nothing to do with the arts, I'm not paying for it.'"

"That's just stupid and mean. How do you expect your kids to succeed if you force them to live in horrible barely surviving conditions?"

"It's ok. It's not that bad here. I'm happy with my mom and stuff," Noelani said, lying to him.

"It's still not fair," he said, in an annoyed tone.

"Yeah, I know. Now come," she said, as she led him to her room.

"Wow, you have a lot of drawings," he said, as he walked in.

"Yes. I do." She took the container from her bag and ate the cupcake. "It's good. Really good."

"That means I'll at least get a B. Thanks."

Noelani gave him back the container and sat back on her bed thinking he'd leave on his own but instead he sat with her.

"Um. Is something wrong?" she asked him

"Can't a guy just sit with his friend?"

"I didn't know we were that kind of friends."

"Of course we are," he said, sounding shocked and maybe offended.

"I thought we were just casual friends. Well actually it's more like acquaintances."

Jake fell silent. Noelani shook her head and started to look up nearby Libraries on her laptop.

"I'll prove it," he finally said. "Tomorrow morning I'll tell my friends."

Noelani looked at him. She wanted to believe him but it was hard to. He was the popular guy,

The Jock, The male lead. Yes, he was kinder than most people who were like him but these titles meant something to him. That's why their friendship had been a secret for the past two years ever since they had Home EC together and were partnered together.

"I'll believe you when it happens," she said carefully.

"Fair enough," he sighed and stood up. "I should be getting home it's late."

"It was late when you got here."

"That is true," he said, grabbing the empty container. "I'll see you tomorrow."

Noelani watched him leave. Then she went back to looking for a new library.

The next morning it was early. Six am early. Noelani had gotten up early to figure out how to get to the library she found last night, but right now sat in the living room drinking a large can of a watermelon monster drink watching the 6 o'clock news, with Alan and Matt.

"Lani sweetheart? What are you doing awake so early?" her mom asked.

"I'm going to check out a new library before school. It's closer than the other one so I'm just trying to wake up."

"You know monster drinks don't work on you anymore. It would be easier to wake up if you were to drink coffee."

"Mom, you know I hate Coffee. I have yet to find a flavor of coffee I can drink."

"I am just saying, we haven't tried every flavor."

"Well not today."

"What's on the news?"

"Alan and Matt are arguing about the simplicity yet complex way of life."

"Ah yes. Well I'm off to work see you later my dear."

"Bye Mom."

An hour later she stood in front of the library she had found the night before. The one-story library stood there with dark blue-green paint. It was definitely smaller than the one in the city. Noelani adjusted the strap of her bag as she walked to the door and read the sign.

"The Mystical Public Library. Open since 1923." *How cute.* She walked to the door and was surprised to find it open so early. Once inside she looked around. To her left was a desk for borrowing books or asking for help. Everywhere else were the books themselves. At the desk sat a beautiful elderly woman with a pixie cut who was sorting through books and organizing them.

"Excuse me?" Noelani asked as she walked over to the desk.

The woman looked up at her and smiled, her blue eyes sparkled gently with intelligence.

"Hello. Welcome to The Mystical Library. How may I help you?" The woman had an English accent.

"Um. Do you have any books on Greek mythology here?" Noelani asked as she read the name tag.

"Yes, we do, right this way please." Julia walked from behind the desk and led the way. "So what brings you here? We don't often see younger people here. They always go to that new bigger library in the center of the city."

"Yeah well. This is actually closer to my house and it's easier to get to," Noelani said as she followed her. "And I've been banned from that one since I can't afford a library card."

"Well, we welcome anyone who enjoys reading, whether you have money or not."

"To be honest, I'm not a big reader. I like listening to music and drawing more but I do like some books. Like this one series based on the Greek and Roman gods. That's why I'm looking for books on the Greek myths so I can learn the origins. I'm also curious about Norse, Egyptian and Celtic myths, but I can't read it all at once so I'm sticking with the Greeks right now."

The librarian stopped and turned to face Noelani. "You are more than welcome to sit here until closing hours and read as much as you want. You can even sit here and draw or listen to your music as long as you have headphones."

"Yes Ma'am. Thank you."

"You are very welcome. Now here we are." The librarian turned around with a gesture to the rounded area they were in. "These are all of our books on mythology. Greek, Roman, Norse. You name it we should have it. There is also a table here so you don't have to go to the tables in front."

"Thank you. I appreciate it."

"You're welcome, I'll be up front if you need me. Enjoy your myths," Julia said with a smile as she walked back to her desk.

Noelani looked through the books hoping to find something that interests her. She had a pile of books picked when she realized it's almost time for school and if she didn't hurry, she would be late. She slid down the latter grabbed her bag and ran but still remembered to say goodbye as she passed the front desk. When she got there, she was completely out of breath panting hard but just in time for her first class. After class she went to her locker to put her books away when someone tickled her from behind making her scream and jump.

Jake chuckled. "Good morning. I told my friends about you."

"What did they say?" Noelani asked, holding back her irritation.

"They want to meet you at lunch," he beamed.

Noelani closed her locker and turned as she shouldered her bag. "I don't think that's a good

Idea. Telling them is one thing but I don't think we would get along very well."

"Please. It's just meeting them. They seem really interested."

Noelani sighed. "Alright, Fine. I'll see you at lunch."

"Great! See you then." Jake walked away.

"Why were you talking to Jake?" Rose said as she approached. "I just saw that whole thing. You were talking to that jerk as if you two were friends."

"Yes, I was because we are friends," Noelani said as she started walking to her class.

"Friends? Since when?" Rose asked following her.

"About two years. Since I first had Home Ec. Together."

"Why didn't you tell me?"

"Because you wouldn't have believed me."

"Yeah, well he has a reputation. What did he want?"

"He finally told his friends that we are friends and they want to meet me at lunch."

"That's not going to end well. What about Samantha?"

"She's always hated me but now she's just learned her boyfriend has been secret friends with the poor girl that she hates. What do you think?"

"I think you should not have lunch with them. It is not going to end well"

"I'm not going to run away from them. They want to meet me. fine. If they bully me. I won't let it bother me. I'll see you after class," Noelani said as she walked in her classroom and sat down making it clear the conversation was over.

Lunch came around and it was the longest thirty minutes she'd ever experienced. His friends were nice enough except for Samantha. Her and Jake had a fifteen minute argument in front of the whole cafeteria. Everyone was silent and their eyes were on either them or Noelani. Then Samantha threw her lunch on her and stormed off. It took another five minutes for Jake to help clean up and the last five minutes she was completely invisible to everyone again except for when Jake would ask if she was ok. She would lie and say she was.

After lunch was over everyone was talking and always glancing at her. Most likely spreading rumors. Then at dance class which she shared with Samantha, it was like Samantha was making it her life's mission to make Noelani mess up. That was the last straw. Once school was finally over. She left as fast as she could. Jake and Rosaline both tried to stop her but she ignored them and just ran. She had no idea where she was going or how long she had been running but when she finally stopped and looked around, she saw the Mystical Library nearby. Being exhausted both physically and emotionally she decided that the library would be a great place to relax for a while.

"Good afternoon, Julia," Noelani said in a bitter tone.

"Are you alright?" Julia asked.

"Yeah, I'm fine," she lied. "I'm just gonna go to the back, I'll see you when I'm ready to leave," Noelani didn't even bother to wait for a response. She just walked back to the mythology section, dropped her bag on the floor, sat at the table and started crying.

Noelani was tired of being bullied. She was tired of being poor. Her father never came by and never helped with anything other than school funds and her brother was off to college. On top of that she was so tired of just barely passing all of her classes. No matter how much she studied nothing ever stuck in her brain long enough to be useful and the only reason she passed at all is because Rose helped her study right before every test. She also hated how she couldn't hold down a job. Her anxiety and memories problems made it hard and she felt bed because she wanted to help.

She was tired of all of this and wished things could be different, or maybe she could be born in a world of magic like her favorite anime, or be a demigod from her favorite book. She could be a beautiful mythical creature like a phoenix, or maybe even a simple house cat since she loved cats. But she knew none of this was possible. Sighing, she sat up and wiped her tears.

After grabbing her books from her bag to start her homework she walked over to the shelves and climbed the ladder to get to the higher books. She reached for a book that didn't have a name on the spine and pulled it out to see the front. It said:

ο κόσμος των ξεχασμένων

Like a lot of books in this section, the cover was in another language. One she recognized as Greek but couldn't understand it, especially since she couldn't read the first part of it due to wear from old age. So she climbed down and grabbed the Greek to English translation book and after twenty minutes she finally figured it out.

She opened it hoping that the words inside were in English for an easy read but all she found were blank pages. "Julia?" she called in confusion.

"Hey, Julia?" she called again and made her way to the front. "Do you know that you have a blank book here?"

When she got to the front desk, she didn't see the librarian there. "Julia?" she looked around some more but she couldn't see her anywhere in the library. *Where did she go;* Noelani thought in confusion. She walked back to the mythology section and looked at the book again as she sat down.

"I see you found the blank book," Julia said from behind Noelani making her jump.

"Jeez, you scared me." Noelani said as she put her hand on her chest.

"My apologies."

"What is this book and why is it blank?" Noelani asked, flipping through the pages again.

"It's just a blank book. I don't know who put it there or why but you are the first person to bring it down since I found it." Julia said.

"Oh. Well, should I put it back?" Noelani asked.

"You don't have to. In fact, I think you should write in it. Try and create your own story, create your own world."

Noelani scoffed "I can't write a book. I can't even write a proper essay or book report."

"That's because you see it as work and work is something you don't want to do. Maybe if you try writing for yourself, you'll find it isn't so bad."

"I don't know," Noelani said with uncertainty.

"Just give it a try. If you don't like it, you can put the book away," Julia encouraged.

"I guess I could try."

Julia smiled. "I'll leave you to it." She pat Noelani on the shoulder before she left. Noelani flipped the book back to the first page then grabbed a pencil from her backpack and stared at the blank paper. She sat there for what seemed like hours having no clue what to write until finally, she thought of a way to start.

She put the tip of the pencil to the paper and wrote. "There once was a girl who lived in a magical land with Kings, Queens, Gods and Goddesses, Demigods, Wizards, Dragons, Fairies and every mythical creature you've ever heard of and possibly more. It was her dream to become a traveler one day; to see the whole world but first, she had to graduate from high school."

When she put the last period there was a sudden blinding bright light coming from the book. Noelani screamed in surprise, dropped her pencil, and covered her face with her arms. Then when the bright light was gone Noelani was no longer sitting in the library.

Chapter 3

"Altalune, Altalune dear it's time to wake up." Noelani opened her eyes and saw a woman with long black hair and crystal blue eyes smiling down at her. "Good morning sleepy head. It's time to get up and get ready for school." The woman stood, "I'm going to finish breakfast."

Noelani watched the woman leave, then looked around confused. The whole room, though small, was covered in pictures of mythical creatures and beautiful scenery. "This isn't the library?" Noelani got out of bed and looked out the window. She saw a bunch of small stone houses with gardens and people moving around setting up shop or going to work, children most likely heading off to school.

"This isn't earth." A dragon flew overhead. "This is definitely not earth." She closed the window and started to look around the room hoping for any signs of where she was when she suddenly remembered what happened. She had started writing in the book when it started to glow. Did she somehow get sucked into the book? Earth didn't have magic. Unless that book wasn't from earth. Either way, Noelani was now stuck here until she could find her way back home.

It took a while to process what was happening. She completely spiraled and curled on the floor struggling to breath but once she accepted that it happened and that there was nothing, she could do about it, she managed to calm down enough to get back up. She went to the closet and found what looked to be a school uniform. She went into the bathroom, did a simple morning routine then looked at herself in the mirror and found she looked different than normal. She had paler skin then she did before, long wavy black hair instead of straight-ish dirty blond and ocean blue eyes instead of blue-gray. She sighed softly and grabbed her backpack as she left her room. She walked down a very short hall, into a small living room where there is a plate of French toast, eggs, fried potatoes, a bowl of fresh fruit and some sort of blue drink.

"It smells amazing," Noelani sighed happily after taking a deep breath.

"Well, I'd hope so. I made your favorite" The woman said, hugging her and kissing her head. Noelani looked at her confused. The woman puts her hand on Noelani's forehead. "Luna dear, are you ok?"

"Umm... I don't know" Noelani said, uncertain of how to answer.

"What's wrong?"

"I don't know who you are. Well. I'm guessing you're my mom"

"Oh dear. How much do you remember?"

"Um...Everything from the moment I woke up."

"Oh dear, Oh Dear!" she said with a worried look. Then gently guided Noelani to the couch. "There have been rumors about children losing their memories. I had hoped that the rumors weren't true"

"I… I'm sorry...mom," Noelani said slowly.

"It's ok sweetie, it's not your fault." The woman smiled as she softly petted Noelani's head. "I guess we should start with the basics. "Your name is Altalune Astra. You are seventeen. Your birthday was yesterday December 5th. Your father left before you were born. You attend a school in the forest for Princesses, Princes, Wizards, and Demigods called Maghi Semidei."

"What am I? Aside from princess. I know I am not a princess," Noelani asked.

"No one is sure. We think you could be a demigod but none of the Gods have claimed you, and monsters don't attack you like they do for most demigods. You are also a descendant of wizards, which is probably because your grandmother was a great wizard and-"

"Do you have magic?" Noelani interrupted.

"No I don't. The ability seems to have skipped a few generations."

"What else can I do?"

"Well, since we think you may be a demigod, we put you in sword practice and archery so you are pretty good at that. You-"

"Why do you keep saying we?" she interrupted again

"Me, your homeroom teacher and the Headmaster of the school. Oh, I should give them a call and tell them what's going on. Eat your breakfast, then you can take Aella to school today since she knows the way."

"Who's Aella?" Noelani asked, sliding off the couch to sit at the table and ate.

"Aella is your Pegasus. You love animals and Aella has been around since you were born. I just found her as a little filly laying by our front door."

"That's cool." Noelani said then continued eating. *My name is Altalune Astra. I think that means over the moon in Latin, Since I'm going to be stuck here for a while. I should accept that. Alright then. From this day forth Noelani Kaneko is no more. I am Altalune, and I have a Pegasus. That's so cool!* She smiled to herself.

Once she was done eating, she took her dishes to the sink, washed them, and then left them to dry on the rack. She hugged her mom goodbye then left the house to find Aella but Aella found her first.

"Good morning," a voice said in her head.

"What the?" Altalune asked, confused.

"Altalune, are you ok?" The voice appeared on her head again. She turned around and saw a beautiful bluish gray Pegasus standing there.

"You can talk?" Altalune asked.

"Not in the same way as you. We can communicate but only you and children of Poseidon can understand me. You've always known this."

"Uhh. Right, well, I don't exactly have my memories."

"Yes, I've been hearing your confusion all morning. No worries, I'm sure you'll remember again soon. For now, you should hop on or you'll be late for school," Aella said, kneeling so Altalune could get on her back.

"Right." She hopped on and Aella took off. "So can you always hear my thoughts?"

"No, not always if I'm far enough away I won't be able to hear your simple thoughts but if you call for me, I'll be able to hear that."

"That's cool." Altalune thought about when she just woke up. "How much of my thoughts did you hear this morning?"

"All of them," Aella said calmly.

"So that means you know," Altalune trailed off when she saw the school building. "It's huge," she said in shock.

"It is a school For Princes, Princesses, Wizards and Demigods what did you expect?"

"I-I don't know," Altalune said nervously.

"Don't be nervous," Aella said. "I know you hate school but you have a best friend that always defends you." Altalune stared with uncertainty at the school as they continue to approach it. It was huge and it looked to be made of the same wood as the trees around it with the roof painted dark green. A black metal gate made a large perimeter around the building.

Inside the perimeter the trees were still green and so was the grass which shouldn't be possible since all around us were clear signs that it was winter. When they landed Altalune could instantly feel the heat and had to take off her jacket before she overheated. As she approached the building, she noticed all the forest animals running around and playing. They must have come over here to escape the cold. She even saw a bear and her cubs playing together. Close to the building was a beautiful garden of flowers.

"This is my school?" Altalune asked.

"Yes."

"How is it so warm?"

"Wizard magic."

"That's so cool, what is the inside like?"

"I don't know, I don't like going inside buildings."

"Makes sense. You are a horse, well not just that but a Pegasus, a wild and free creature. So do I just walk in or-" Altalune started but a new voice; not in her head, interrupted her.

Chapter 4

"Hey, Altalune!!" A girl said as she ran over from the building. "You're here. I was starting to think you were going to be late."

"Um, hi..." Altalune said nervously. The girl in front of her had short choppy brown hair, dark eyes, lips as red as roses and skin almost as white as the snow outside the parimiture.

"Are you ok Lune?" she asked.

"Um. Yeah, I just don't have my memories anymore."

Her friend gasped. "No way, do you know what this means?"

"Um..." Altalune looked around confused. "No. what does it mean?"

"It means that you are one of the ones in the prophecy."

"A prophecy?" Altalune said slowly as she thought about her dream the other night. "As in from the gods?"

"Yes. In fact, the rumors say that this prophecy came from Apollo himself!"

Altalune looks up at the sky, the sun just barely peeking over the trees. "Um. So what is the prophecy?"

"That is something we must discuss privately," said a voice coming from behind the girl. Both girls looked and saw an old man standing there. He had a small beard and mustache, messy hair and was wearing a robe like something you see in movies. "Roxanne, please go to class."

"Yes, Headmaster Charles. Bye Lune," Roxanne said then left.

"Come with me," Headmaster Charles said then turned around and walked into the building. Altalune followed.

The inside was definitely way, way bigger than on the outside. The entrance was two huge beautifully carved wooden doors that lead to a massive foyer. All around students were gathered in groups talking and smiling, or sitting and studying or comparing notes. Some girls were giggling and putting makeup on. Some boys were practicing sword fighting. Some with bronze and golden swords. Some with normal metal swords. Altalune guessed the ones using bronze and gold swords were Demigods but that was just a guess.

There were also some students who had pets. Some as simple as white owls, eagles, or cats and some a bit more exotic like a fiery phoenix.

There were also students practicing magic. One of them had cast some sort of spell but it failed with a burst of air sending papers spiraling to the ceiling that had a large, beautiful crystal glass chandelier. At the end of the foyer were two staircases leading to the second floor.

"To the left are the girl dorms, to the right the boy dorms," Headmaster Charles said as they got to the center of the foyer. "There are fifty on each side and three floors."

"So there're three hundred students?" Altalune asked as they scale the stairs. "How many of them are demigods?"

"Only a third of the students here are demigods. There are more in other schools but it still doesn't add up too much. Many demigod children don't survive past their eighteenth birthday," he said as they walked down the hall.

Altalune thought about how she just turned seventeen and how her mother said she suspected she was a demigod. Which meant it was possible she would die very soon.

"That's sad," she looked around. "Where are we going?"

"The fourth floor." Headmaster Charles opened a door that led to more stairs.

"Fourth floor?" Altalune asked as she peaked over the railing of the spiral staircase and looked up. "That's a lot of stairs."

"This staircase leads straight to the fourth floor." Headmaster Charles said as he continued to walk. "It makes for good work out," he said in a humorous tone.

"And a good way to be sore in the morning," Altalune mumbled and followed.

After about twenty minutes they made it to the top. They would have gotten there in ten but Altalune had to half carry, half drag the headmaster after his back gave out halfway up. She pushed the door open then gently sat him in the first thing she saw, a golden chair.

"Are you ok?" she asked worriedly.

"Yes, I'm fine, I just need some rest."

"Headmaster Charles!" A voice comes from somewhere else on the floor followed by multiple running footsteps. Altalune looked in the direction of the voice but got distracted by the room filled with different things displayed all around. *This must be why he didn't count the fourth floor when counting the students.* Altalune thought.

"Headmaster Charles, are you ok?" A boy with sandy blonde hair knelt in front of the headmaster.

"Yes, I'm fine Ted. You don't need to worry about me," Headmaster Charles said, groaning a little. "I just need some rest. Would you take Altalune and the others to the scroll and explain Everything?"

"Yes Sir. You can count on me," Ted said confidently. He looked at Altalune with his sky blue eyes. "Come the prophecy is this way," he then turned and led the way to the back of the room. There was a girl with long curly golden blond hair waiting not too far away. She glared at Altalune then flipped her hair as she turned around and hugged Ted's arm as she followed him, leaving Altalune alone with the now sleeping headmaster and a little boy that was also there staring up at her.

Altalune sighed. "My first day of school and someone already hates me."

"She's just jealous of you," the little boy said.

"Jealous why?" Altalune asked, confused.

"Well, I guess it started about a month ago," he started. "At least that's what I remember since that day was the first day of school for me after I lost my memories."

"We should probably follow them while you tell me," Altalune suggested.

The little boy nodded and started walking, leaving Altalune to follow. "There aren't many kids my age in this school so most of my classes are on the first floor so I don't get super lost because this school is huge. It's also where the gym is. I was on my way to one of my classes when I heard a loud voice from inside the gym. I peeked inside and saw Eleanor accusing you of trying to take Ted from her."

"So her name is Eleanor?" Altalune asked. "It kinda suits her."

The boy nodded. "You told her that you weren't trying to steal Ted, you were just training with him since the coach paired you two against each other but she didn't believe you. She went on and on about how you weren't pretty or special until finally, you snapped. There was a contest to see who was the fairest of them all and you said something like 'you know what Eleanor. I'll enter The FTA contest and when I fail it'll prove that I don't want your boyfriend and I'm not trying to steal him.' Elenore agreed and you two went on with your day."

"That sounds like something I would say. Then what happened?" Altalune asked.

"Since the contest went on past my bedtime, I don't know everything but apparently you won."

"Wait really?" Altalune asked surprised.

"Yeah, according to what the other students said you were average on the intelligence test your ballroom dancing was something you could work on but your freestyle was what caught the Judges attention."

"Huh? What could I have possibly done to make up for failing the first two tests?" Altalune asked. *I'm not surprised my ballroom dancing needed work. I was out sick for half the lesson I think it was...* "There's different types of ballroom dancing, what was it?"

"I think it was the waltz but I don't really know. All I know is you won and she hates you more for it."

"Well that's just lovely," Altalune said sarcastically. *It was definitely the waltz that I missed in school.*

"So there was no beauty test?"

"No, the contest is just something for fun to ease stress. Well it is supposed to do that."

"And girls like Eleanor makes it not so fun." Altalune sighed.

They caught up to Ted and Eleanor in front of the back wall that is a floor to ceiling end to end bookshelf with many many books and scrolls. In front of the bookshelf stood a pedestal with a glass box. There was a simple scroll tied with a simple red ribbon that hovered inside.

"It's about time. You two are so slow," Elenore complained.

"Sorry. I was just telling Altalune about your failure in the FTA contest." The boy said with a little sass.

"Nick you little brat I told you not to tell her!" Eleanor snapped.

"I don't have to take orders from you, meanie!" Nick said, as he stuck his tongue out at her.

"Why you little brat!" Eleanor tried to grab him but Altalune stepped in between them, forcing her to stop. "Out of my way!"

"Compose yourself Elenore. You are about to hear the prophecy," Ted said and lifted the glass box off the pedestal.

The scroll rolled open on its own and shone brightly. Then a sparkly golden image of a handsome god floated there. "Hello? Is this thing on? Hephaestus, is this thing working?"

"Yes Apollo, it's working, will you just get this over with and get out of my workshop," Hephaestus said in a very annoyed tone towards his nephew.

"Alright alright." Apollo grinned "Hello humans and fans of me!"

"Apollo" Hephaestus' voice rose making it clear his patients was running low.

"Right the prophecy. What was it again? Oh Yeah."

> **"Those for whom a past they lack,**
> **Must then walk a certain track,**
> **To find a whom or thing they need,**
> **So their memories bloom like a seed."**

"Hmm. That sounds boring and drab. Oh I know I'll sing it!" Apollo said beaming as his lyur appeared in his hands.

"That's it! Get out!" Hephaestus said, then the image disappeared and the scroll floated back to the pedestal and Ted put the box back over it.

Chapter 5

"That was Apollo?" Altalune asked surprised and confused.

"He's so dreamy," Eleanor said in awe.

Altalune, Ted and Nick rolled their eyes.

"What! He is!" Eleanor whined.

Ted shook his head. "This has been the prophecy for five years. Three students of this school lost their memory the same day it arrived and three more lost their memories the year after and again on the next. You three are the thirteenth." He pointed to Eleanor "Fourteenth." Pointed to Nick "And fifteenth," he pointed to Altalune. "Person who's lost their memories."

"Why so many?" Altalune asked. "Hasn't anyone tried following the prophecy?"

"Yes, every person who has lost their memories has tried to find who or what they need but we've all turned up with nothing."

"What do you mean by we? Have you lost your memories too?" Altalune asked.

"No, but since we are dealing with lost memories, Headmaster Charles wanted one person with memories to help guide them. That person has been me," Ted said. "Also since you just lost your memories, you're going to need some time to get used to things again."

Altalune stared around the room thinking. "No. I can worry about getting used to things after everything is said and done. Where's the Library? Maybe there's something someone else missed-"

"Wow Altalune to the rescue, how surprising" Eleanor said sarcastically. "Do you really think you can find something twelve other people have tried to find when you have no clues just like the rest of us."

"At least I came up with something. What have you been doing this whole time?"

"Ladies," Ted said firmly to stop the bickering.

"I think there is a small possibility that the Four of us can find something together if you're willing to get your hands dirty and help with all the old smelly dusty books," Altalune continued.

"You didn't say all of us," Eleanor complained.

"That's what happens when you don't let someone finish." Altalune said.

"Keep your claws in girls. We are wasting time. Let's get to the library. The sooner we look the better." Ted told them calmly.

Altalune nodded as Eleanor huffed.

"Can I help!" Nick asked.

"Of course, You are one of the people who lost their memories so you are a part of this too. Come on," Ted said and led the way back to the front.

"Yes!" Nick ran after him.

Altalune giggled softly and followed. "So what is this place anyway?" She asked, as she looked around ignoring Eleanor's cries of complaint.

"Oh this floor is like a mini-museum," Nick said.

"It's actually a storage space for legendary items. For example, the chair you set the headmaster in; that was king Midas' throne," Ted said.

"If that's king Midas's throne what's it doing so close to the stairs like tha—" She paused in the middle of her sentence as she thought about the narrow stairs she climbed up. "Wait, how did they even get it up here in the first place?"

Ted chuckled. "It was very difficult and once it was up here no one wanted to move it around this large room until they found 'the perfect spot' for it so they just left it there."

"If king Midas was here, he would not be happy," Altalune said, trying to imagine the king's reaction and she giggled at her own imagination.

"No, he wouldn't," Ted agreed. "Luckily he's been dead for years.

The four of them go back to the first floor and then to the library. Ted and Nick started gathering the books. Anything that could possibly be useful while Altalune sat at a table going through them and Eleanor sat in a bean bag chair filling her nails. Hours past the school bell rang but they didn't leave; they continued to look through the books, before they realized it; it was Midnight.

Altalune rubbed her face and looked at the large clock on the wall chiming. " I can't believe we've been here all day. Shouldn't someone at least take Nick home?" She asked, looking at the twelve year old boy asleep on a pile of books.

"It's alright. I called his mother earlier, she's fine with him staying here as long as he's taken care of," Ted said as he walks over picked up the boys blazer off the floor and put it over him like a blanket.

"I should have thought to call my mom," Altalune said, dropping her head on the book she was reading.

Ted chuckled softly. "It's ok. I called her for you." He slipped off his Blazer and put it over her shoulders.

"Why?" she asked in a sleepy tone.

"Because I'm a prince. It's my job to make sure everyone is taken care of and there are no problems."

Altalune lifted her head and looked at him. "Prince?"

"Yeah. Prince Ted Miller, descendant of Alexander the great, at your service," he said as he smiled charmingly.

"Does that mean Eleanor is a princess?" She asked, as she looked around for her but it seems she had left.

"No. She's the descendant of Goldilocks but no one knows who her father is."

"What about Nick?"

"His parents are human. They take care of the Hades temple in town. He was chosen by Hades himself to take care of his youngest son here at school but Hades' son tends to ditch him because he'd rather be alone and now that his memories are gone, he doesn't remember what he looks like so hasn't been able to find him."

"Do you-" She started to ask but yawned before she could finish.

"Why. don't you get some sleep. We can continue looking in the morning," Ted suggested.

Altalune was too tired to complain so she just rested her head back on the book and quickly fell asleep. This was her first time sleeping in this world and her first dream made no sense to her at all. The first thing she saw was a small old building with two small dragon statues sitting on either side of the door. Well compared to the dragon she saw flying over her house when she first got here, they were small but they were still the size of cars.

The scene changed to her standing in front of a bookshelf staring at a book with two torches crossing on the spine. Then she was in a long dark hallway. Running towards some stairs as the room shook around her. Everything went dark when she suddenly woke up to screaming. She stood up quickly in a panic then she realized it was just Eleanor and she collapsed back into her chair.

"What do you want?" Altalune groaned as she rubbed her face.

"The only person who should be wearing Teddy's blazer is me!" Eleanor snapped as she took it from the floor.

"Eleanor. It's my blazer if I put it on someone to keep them warm then that's my choice," Ted groaned in annoyance.

"I am your girlfriend not her." Eleanor stated as she put it on.

Ted sighed in defeat and stood up. "I'll get breakfast from the school cafeteria," he left the room and Altalune went back to reading the book she had slept on but she wasn't really reading. She saw the words but didn't really process what it was saying.

When Ted came back, they enjoyed their food quietly. After breakfast they went back to work. Altalune's friend Roxanne came by a few hours later and asked if she could help too. They gratefully accepted but by lunchtime Roxanne and Nick had given up completely.

"My head hurts," Roxanne complained.

"Can we please stop," Nick whined.

"Reading this much is not good for my complexion," Eleanor said, while she looked at herself in her hand mirror.

"Like you have been doing much reading," Altalune sighed, she closed the book in front of her and added it to one of the piles of other books around her. She pressed her hands against her forehead due to the pounding pain. "We can break for lunch then we need to get back to work. Is there a magical way to cure headaches?" she asked with weak hope.

"Yeah, I know a guy, I'll go get him," Roxanne said then left the library.

"I'll go get lunch from the cafeteria," Ted said and walked to the door as someone else walked in. He had messy black hair and milky white skin. He clearly didn't care about the school uniform because instead of that he had on a black leather jacket over a white shirt, black jeans with holes designed to be there, a gold chain hooked on the belt loops, front to back, black leather boots and a sword at his waist.

Ted stopped in front of the man. "Why are you here?"

"Nick's mom asked me to bring this to him." The mystery boy said and put a lunch bag on the table in front of Nick. His voice was captivating and Altalune couldn't help but stare at the handsome boy.

"Thanks," Nick said, taking his lunch.

"Who are you?" Altalune asked.

"This is Damon Nuovo, Son of Hades and the strongest demigod in this school," Eleanor said.

"You are the boy I'm supposed to watch over!" Nick said in surprise.

"You mean the jerk who keeps ditching you?" Altalune said as she sat crossed legged on the table she's been reading at and stared up at the dark-haired boy, his golden, shattered glass eyes stared down at her, almost challenging her. Daring her to question his strength but there was something else in his eyes that she couldn't quite place. Hesitation? Fear? Whatever it was she knew this was definitely a man who didn't like to show weakness.

She held out her hand. "My name is Altalune. It's nice to meet you." She smiled sweetly. He continued to stare with a cold expression. "Well. Thank you for bringing Nick's lunch," she put her hand back down. "You may leave now since you clearly don't care that the young boy will no doubt be going on a dangerous mission with his memories gone or maybe you're just too scared to come. "

"Don't say that." Eleanor hissed.

"I don't fear anything," Damon growled angrily, his voice still captivating to her.

It took a second for Altalune to gather her thoughts again. "Now that's a complete lie. Everyone is afraid of something. Like me, I hate certain types of bugs. I'll screech if they come anywhere near me unexpectedly."

"That's a dumb fear" Damon said annoyed tone.

"So? It's a fear and it's a fear I'm slowly working on getting over. If I see one and it's far enough away. I won't screech." She stood and slowly started circling him. "You refuse to face your fears. You would rather stay here safe and protected in the walls of the school. That tells me you are nothing more than a coward hiding behind a facade of strength." She gently slid back onto the table keeping the soft smile on her face.

"You don't know me," Damon growled. A dark aura slowly spreading from him.

"Then you wouldn't mind coming with us on our mission to protect the young boy who was chosen to watch over you."

"I don't need someone to watch over me I am not weak. He's weak." Damon tone slowly got louder and angrier.

"Hey!" Nick complained about Damon's comment.

"Did it ever occur to you that maybe your father wanted you to have a friend." Altalune swung her legs. "Someone for you to care for and to care for you? Maybe because you don't get along with anyone your father feels bad that you're so alone and that's why he sent this boy to 'watch over' you?"

Damon stared at her. "I don't need anyone but myself." He turned and walked out of the library. Passing Roxanne on the way and a boy.

"Was that Damon?" she asked, "As in super hot son of Hades, Damon?"

"Yeah, and Altalune basically just called him out on being heartless," Nick said.

"And you're alive?" Roxanne asked, poking Altalune's ribs causing her to squirm.

"Yes, I'm alive! That tickles!"

"Well, this is Nigel. He's a sky wizard which includes a few different things including healing," Roxanne said in a bragging tone.

"Alright. I've already healed Rox so who's next," Nigel asked.

" Do Nick next," Altalune said.

Nigel nodded then walked over to Nick and gently put his hands on Nick's head. "So how's the search coming?" he asked as he worked.

"Not very well," Ted said with a heavy sigh.

"That's a bummer," Nigel said without opening his eyes.

"If only we had some sort of clue aside from the prophecy," Roxanne said as she sat on a pile of books.

"Wait…" Altalune froze when she started to remember her dream. The two golden dragon statues the torch cross on the spin of the book. "That's It!" She said loudly. She hopped off the table ran to one of the book piles near the table

Ted had been working at and started looking through said books.

Chapter 6

"That is it?" Ted asked.

"Ignore her," Eleanor complained.

"This entire time we've been looking for someone or something," she opened a book "but we should have been looking for both." and started flipping through the pages.

"I don't get it," Roxanne said, confused.

"If I'm remembering this right" She mumbles, "Here!" She points to a page in the book 'Medea is a descendant of the Titan Helios, the niece of the sorceress Circe and a priestess of Hecate, Medea was a powerful sorceress renowned for her healing skills and proficiency in using herbs and drugs." Altalune read. "This is what we're looking for."

"How?" Eleanor asked. "She's just a wizard. If that's what we're looking for we would have finished this already."

"Medea is not a wizard, there's a difference and I bet if she was here, she'd be insulted. A wizard and a sorceress are very different." Altalune said.

"Then tell me old wise one, what is the difference?" Eleanor said sarcastically.

"That's something I can't explain since I'm neither a wizard nor sorceress," Altalune said, sighing.

"Well you could be one," Ted said because your grandmother was one and you've done a few spells. Granted not successfully but still."

"Whatever. Either way, I can't tell you since I don't remember but something is telling me I'm right on this. We find Medea, we find the cure," Altalune said confidently.

"Medea has been dead for years," Ted said.

"It doesn't have to be Medea herself, maybe a decedent, a pupil, a shrine or something!" Altalune said.

"I think there's a shrine to Medea in the town not too far from here," Nick said.

"Then we start there," Ted said as he stood up. "But we'll fly over the rest of the forest since it's dangerous to pass the school borders."

"How? not all of us have Pegasus like Altalune." Nick asked.

"We'll take Aiden," Ted said.

"Who's Aiden?" Altalune asked.

"Aiden is my dragon friend. I found him when he was a baby and nursed him back to health. He's the only dragon of his kind left in existence." Ted said sadly.

"Dragons are extinct? That's sad."

"Can we go now? I really want to meet the dragon. Please." Nick begged.

Ted chuckled and ruffled his hair. "Not yet we need to tell the headmaster our plans then we need to prepare for the journey. You can meet Aiden tomorrow."

"Ok." Nick pouted.

After they ate lunch. Ted left the library to talk to the headmaster and Eleanor followed him to get out of putting away all the books. Nick tried to as well but Altalune wouldn't let him, saying that they shouldn't leave such a big mess for the librarian to clean up on her own. By the time that was done the bell rang for the end of school and they all went home to get some rest. In the morning instead of going to school they met at the palace where Ted already had bags prepared for them. Everyone was standing around waiting. Dressed and prepared for traveling except for Eleanor who looked like she was ready for her close up to be on the cover of some magazine.

"Am I late," Altalune asked.

"No. just in time," Ted said, then handed her a bag. "There's food and water to last a few days, some money in case we need it and first aid."

"Thanks." Altalune knelt and took everything out so she could rearrange it all to be able to fit the change of clothes and few other things her mother had packed for her in her own bag.

"We're just going to another town, why do we need so much?" Eleanor complained.

"We never know what could happen on a quest so it's better safe than sorry. Also, this is for you." Ted handed Altalune something wrapped in cloth.

Altalune shouldered her bag then gently took it and unwrapped the cloth around it. She found a sword in a normal leather sheath. She took the handle of the sword and pulled it out.

"I know it probably won't feel right but I hope it's a better fit and more comfortable for you to use then the training swords in school," Ted said.

"I don't know how to use a sword," Altalune said slowly studying the blade.

"You do. Trust me"

"Ok, thank you," she said then tied the sword to her waist.

"You're welcome." Ted suddenly made a really loud whistle which made Altaluna flinch. Then after a few minutes they heard a roar. A yellow orange dragon came into view, it was almost the color of a tangerine. It landed in the vast courtyard where they were standing in then nuzzled Ted causing the prince to chuckle as he stumbled back a little and petted the dragon's snout. "This is Aiden the only dragon left in the world."

"He's so cool!" Nick said in awe like any twelve-year old boy who loves dragons would. "Can I pet him please, please, please?" He asked, dragging out the last, please.

"Yes, he's friendly but you need to let him sniff you first so stand very still," Ted said, then looked at Aiden. Aiden sniffed Eleanor first then sneezed blowing smoke all around her making her cough. Next it was Nick's turn. Nick squirmed and giggled as the dragon poked his nose in the little boy's stomach.

Finally, Aiden turned his attention to Altalune. After dealing with many stray, scared, and aggressive animals back in the normal world she knew to stay still, keep her fear at bay, stay calm, relaxed, and have patients otherwise she may scare the animal and she does just that until Aiden starts growling. Panic started to rise in her but she continued to stay still knowing if she moved it could end badly.

"Aiden, no she's a friend," Ted said, getting between her and his dragon. "Don't hurt her."

Aiden continued to stare at Altalune and as she stared back shaking as she tried to stay calm, she can see her reflection in its blood orange eyes. But instead of Altalune's features, she saw the familiar features of her true self. Who she was outside this world? The scared little girl who couldn't do anything right. Determined, she closed her eyes and pushed her fear down. Then she held the dragon's stare until he finally turned away from her. She sighed and fell to her knees her hands shaking due to the level of anxiety she was feeling. Her chest was so tight that she felt she couldn't breathe.

"I'm so sorry he's only ever done that with…" Ted's voice trailed off not wanting to finish his sentence but she knew what he meant. Aiden has only growled at enemies and now saw her as one. "Are you ok?" Ted asked and helped her up.

"Yeah, I'm fine. Thank you," Altalune said and dust herself off. "I'm a stranger, not everyone likes a person at the first meeting. I'll just ride Aella."

"Yeah. Alright." He turned away from her and picked up his bag. "Let's get going. I want to get there before nightfall." Ted climbed onto Aiden's back. Elenore huffed and climbed on behind him then Nick looked at Altalune sadly before grabbing his and Eleanor's bag and joining them. Aiden took off leaving Altalune standing by herself.

"Don't let the dragon's reaction get to you," Aella's voice said in her head, making Altalune jump.

"Jeez don't sneak up on people," Altalune said.

"My Apologies." Aella said. "I just heard you say you needed me."

Altalune sighed and grabbed her bag before climbing onto the Pegasus. "It's ok. I'm just worried."

"Don't be," Aella said, taking off. "He just knows your different"

"Can every animal tell?" Altalune asked.

"Yes, but it's ok. I know you belong here and that you are a good person at heart," Aella said with such confidence Altalune couldn't help but smile.

They silently fly through the sky. Altalune looked down and watched the forest pass far below her. She slowly and carefully stood up trying her best not to hurt Aella as well as keep her balance with her arms spread. Her hair dancing in the wind, she took a deep breath then let herself fall backward. She didn't panic. Her heart didn't race. Fear didn't rise within her. She just straightened her body hugging herself and just let herself fall. As if on instinct she reached in front of her and wrapped her arm around something. She felt herself spin then swoop up before steadying into a glide again. She opened her eyes she found herself back in the position she started in. Sitting on Aella.

"What do you think you're doing? You could get hurt!" Aella said in a scolding tone.

"Sorry. I don't know why I just felt like doing it."

"Well next time warn me. I just barely missed the trees," Aella said, flapping her wings getting a little higher.

"Alright I will." She promised.

"Will You stop talking to your horse? It's weird!" Elenore complained.

Altalune sighed and stared at the horizon, then looked at her hands and they were shaking again. *I have to stay calm*. She thought to herself. *I have to be strong. I have to be Altalune, not Noelani.* She held her hands together and just watched the world around them. Once they reached the town Nick, Eleanor and Ted slid off Aiden's back and down his tail since the dragon was too big to land anywhere in town and Altalune hopped off Aella.

"So Nick, do you know where this temple of Medea is?" Ted asked.

"If there is even a temple to some wizard," Eleanor said.

"Sorceress not wizard." Altalune corrected only to get an eye roll in response.

"The temple of Medea is here," Nick said. "I should know, us temple keepers stay in touch with each other. My mom said the temple is on the west side of the town. Which side are we on?" he asked.

"We are on the southeast side so the temple is somewhere that way." Ted said pointing northwest.

"Then let's get walking. We only have a few hours of daylight left," Altalune said.

"Yeah, we know that," Eleanor said, her voice dripping with attitude as she hugged Ted's arm and glared daggers at Altalune.

"Eleanor how many times do I have to tell you not to be rude," Ted scolded her.

"But she's the-" Eleanor started to complain.

"Altalune is not the enemy!" Ted snapped. "I may not know her much but we do talk occasionally and I know she is a nice girl. Aiden was just being cautious."

Elenore stared at him in shock and Altalune smiled softly, relieved he believed in her and she had a friends. The four of them start walking towards the northwest side of town. By the time they found the temple it was almost completely dark. Altalune instantly recognized the two golden dragon statues at the door that shined in the last light of day. Nick walked in first with confidence. Ted and Eleanor pass through second but Altalune didn't follow them.

She stared at the Dragons, something told her they weren't just statues. She slowly studied them and when her eyes met with the glowing orange eyes of the left dragon, it finally hit her. Those were Medea's sun dragons. She watched as they started to move creeping closer. Their mouths opened just enough that as they hissed, she could see the flames in the back of their throats.

Altalune just stood there paralyzed because that's what happens when you look into their eyes just as they were close enough for her to feel the heat radiating from their skin, there was a flash of movement and the two dragons crumble to dust. Altalune gasped softly in surprise and looked up to see Ted standing over the piles.

"Are you crazy?" He snapped. "Those things were going to kill you!"

"Those were Medea's sun dragons," Altalune said softly, "but I didn't realize it until after I was paralyzed from looking into their eyes."

"Jeez you're going to get yourself killed," Ted said and put his sword away. "I've never seen dragons like that."

"They were a gift to Medea from her grandfather Helios. It makes sense that they were guarding her temple," Altalune said as they walked to the door where Nick and Eleanor were watching.

"But why did they react to you and not the rest of us?" Nick asked.

"The same reason Aiden growled at her," Eleanor said. "She's bad news."

"That's enough, I don't want to talk about it anymore. We should find a place to get some rest and come back in the morning," Ted said.

"I saw what looked to be an inn over that way." Altalune pointed to the direction with her thumb.

"Alright let's go," Ted said and led the way.

Chapter 7

When they got to the building that Altalune said she thought was an inn they found out that it was more of a fancy restaurant. Everything on the inside sparkled and looked like it was made of pure crystal.

"I guess I was wrong," Altalune said in awe.

"Yeah, you were." Eleanor was far too awestruck to even trying to sound sarcastic.

"That's ok. We can eat here and ask for directions to the inn when we're done," Ted said.

"Yay! I'm starving!" Nick said.

A girl about fourteen years of age walked over to them. Her hair had three different colors: dark purple at the roots, dark green in the middle and light green tips fading perfectly together. "Good evening welcome to The Rainbow Phoenix Guild. How many people will be dining with us tonight?" The girl said in a very professional tone for someone so young. Even Altalune wasn't able to figure out how to sound professional and sweet at the same time.

"Just four," Ted said in response.

"Right this way please." She grabbed four menus then led the way. Deeper in the restaurant. "My name is Calla and I'll be your waitress tonight."

"But you said Rainbow Phoenix guild. By guild do you mean wizard guild?" Altalune asked.

"Yes. The staff here are all wizards. The owner is our master Marco. We run this place like a restaurant as a kind of extra work for when wizards want to take a break from magic quests. That way we can still make some money as we rest." Calla said then stopped at a booth table. "Here you go." She put the menus down as the four of them sat down. "I'll come back soon to take your orders." She bowed politely then walked away.

Once they order, they ate and talked about the mission constantly going back and forth on what could or couldn't happen. "Why are we even talking about this? We know where to look. All we need to do is find the thing that'll bring back our memories and boom we're done," Eleanor said.

"It's too easy, that's the problem there's gotta be something else we're missing," Altalune argued.

"Maybe there is going to be some sort of test we have to pass once we're inside?" Ted suggested.

"Excuse me. I know I shouldn't intervene but did I hear you say, 'get your memories back'?" Calla asked.

"Yeah, Eleanor, Nick and Altalune have lost their memories," Ted said, "why do you ask?"

"I've lost my memories too. It happened a few weeks ago."

"What was your name again?" Altalune asked.

"My name is Calla. I specialize in plant magic but I'm trying to learn all sorts of things."

"Well that could be helpful," Altalune said as she looked at her friends.

"Absolutely not!" Eleanor said firmly.

"It's not your choice," Altalune said calmly as she looked at Ted. "You're the team leader."

"Let's put it to a vote. Who thinks it's a good idea for Calla to come?" Ted said, raising his hand. Altalune and Nick rose their hands as well. "Three against one, looks like you're coming with us," Ted said as he stood up. "Take me to your guild Master so I can explain everything."

"Thank you so much!" Calla said happily then led the way to the back.

After Ted talked to the guild master Calla took them to her small apartment where the four of them crashed for the night. Nick then woke them up at the break of dawn to get ready and get going.

"Come on guys, we need to go," Nick said, pulling the blanket off of Ted.

Ted sat up yawning, Eleanor groaned something about needing beauty sleep, Calla got up with no problems and Altalune just laid there in her spot not moving. It wasn't until everyone else was awake and ready did they realize she was still asleep.

"Why does she get to sleep in?" Eleanor complained.

"Ooops. I forgot to wake her up," Nick said, feeling guilty that he forgot her.

"It's ok, I got it," Ted said, then walked over to Altalune, kneeled next to her, and gently shook her. "Altalune It's time to wake up." Ted said softly.

Altalune groaned and lifted her head. She looked around her messy hair falling into her face then looked up at the window. "The sun isn't even out yet." She groaned and covered her head with blanket as she laid back down.

Ted chuckled, gently removed the blanket, took her hands, and pulled her up. She wobbled and Ted had to hold her so she didn't fall. "You ok?"

"Yeah, I'm fine." She yawned and rubbed her eyes. "Why are we getting up so early?"

"Because if we're early we won't have to wait in line to get in," Nick said.

"Like there is going to be a line at a creepy temple for someone who isn't even a god," Eleanor said while she rolled her eyes.

"At least you didn't call her a wizard again." Altalune sighed, grabbing her bag, and pulling out a hairbrush.

"Hey what's wrong with Wizards?" Calla asked.

"Nothing, it's just Medea is not a wizard she's a sorceress there's a difference," Altalune said then walked to the bathroom.

"Oh yeah there's a huge difference." Calla agreed.

"What is this difference?" Elenore asked again.

"No one knows for sure it's just every wizard who studies magic is told from a very young age that there's a difference. It's just one of those things the people have just accepted without asking questions." Calla explained.

"Well there has to be a difference otherwise it wouldn't be a big deal," Eleanor said, annoyed.

"Look, that's not important right now. We need to focus on trying to find whom or what we need to get our memories back," Altalune said coming back out.

"Altalune is right, let's go," Ted said and led the way.

When they got to the small run-down temple. The sun dragon's posts were still empty.

"We should hurry. The sun dragons should have reformed by now so they'll show up at any moment," Ted said, looking around cautiously, his hand on his sword.

"Woah! Dragons can reform?" Calla asked in awe.

"Not all dragons, the sun dragons that were here before can reform but the dragons that went extinct those can't," Ted said.

"Oh?" Calla said, confused. "What's the difference?" She asked as they followed Altalune and Ted into the Temple.

"The difference other than size and a few minor features is the dragons that went extinct were around before even the gods. At least that's what legend said no one knows for sure," Ted said as he looked around the small room. All the walls are built-in bookshelves with dust-covered books.

"This looks more like an abandoned bookstore instead of a shrine," Eleanor said, looking disgusted.

"I don't understand," Nick said, sad and confused.

"Let's look around, maybe we can find some clues," Altalune said and everyone split up to examine the books and items that were there. After a while she wandered further into the back. She was sensing something she didn't understand. Some sort of power. Dark but not evil. Altalune ran her finger along the books.

Then stopped at a single book. There were no words but at the very top of the spine was a single design. Two crossed torches in gold. Just like her dream.

She gently pulled the book and heard something click. Then the bookshelves separated revealing a staircase leading downward into darkness.

"Cool! A secret passage!" Nick said coming from behind her.

Ted, Eleanor, and Calla walked over and looked down the stairs.

"There is no way I'm going down there," Eleanor said, crossing her arms.

"Fine you say here," Ted said. "Keep watch."

"I'll lead the way," Altalune said and started walking. Calla followed behind her.

"Nick stay here and Keep Elenore company," Ted said.

"I don't want to stay here with her, she's mean!" Nick complained.

Ted crouched down to his height. " I need you to stay here in case someone tries to follow us. I want you to stop them in any way you can. Ok?" He asked quietly so only Nick could hear him. "Do you think you can do that?"

Nick nodded with determination. Ted ruffled Nick's hair then followed Altalune and Calla. The stairs seemed to go down forever. It was completely dark except for the soft firelight Calla was making with her magic allowing Altalune to see one step ahead of her and it was so narrow that they had no choice but to walk single file. The only thing they could hear was their footsteps. They eventually made it to the bottom that led into a very long hallway with doors on either side going all the way down. Like something you would find in a hotel. The same thing she saw in her dream. With Altalune still leading the way they walk down the hall in silence.

The doors were made of old dark wood, each door had two torches on either and brass numbers at eye level. Altalune stopped at a seemingly random door, the number on it read 1819 and the brass had turned green from oxidation and lack of cleaning. She opened the door, not even hesitating and walked in. As soon as the door opened the room was lit up by magic torches lined along the walls. The first thing they noticed was a giant birdcage in the middle of what looked like a bedroom with floor to ceiling bookshelves and a desk.

In the cage was someone sitting, watching them approach. She had long dark hair that was a complete mess with bangs that covered her eyes. Her clothes were dirty and she looked like she hadn't been eating properly for months. Altalune walked closer to the cage and the girl backed away in fear.

"It's OK, I'm not here to hurt you, I want to help you," Altalune said in a soft voice.

"You knew she was in here?" Ted asked.

"Kind of, it was like I could sense her," Altalune said, trying to figure out how to open the cage. She eventually found a key under one of the books that were stacked on the desk and used it to unlock the cage door and went inside. Once inside a bright yellowish light surrounds the cage. Altalune turned around confused, she tried to leave but hit a barrier. She cursed in pain then looked at Calla. "I think it's magic."

Chapter 8

Calla walked over and put her hands on the barrier wall. It shimmered a dull yellow at her touch. A purple aura shone around her hands as she closed her eyes, mumbling softly. The light from her hands got brighter and brighter, reflecting off the barrier as she struggled to bring it down before long it was so bright the others had to look away. They heard a scream and the light faded. Ted looked up and saw Calla had been thrown across the room and hit the wall near the door. Where two girls were now standing and giggling.

"Please, your so-called magic power has nothing against true magic," One of the girls said she had short choppy brown hair with dark green tips, Emerald green eyes, a forest green tank top under a military jacket, short shorts and Combat boots. She also had a necklace around her neck and the charm shined gently in the soft fire light. Altalune recognized it as Hecate's wheel.

"Who are you?" Ted said, drawing his sword.

"Ted don't," Altalune said firmly. "We aren't here to cause trouble. Can you please let us go?"

"You caused trouble the second you trespassed on our property. This is for children of Hecate only." The girl with choppy hair said.

"How did you even get down here? This place is hidden," The girl next to her said she had dark skin and curly blond hair.

"I just followed my instincts. Look all we want is a potion to help memory loss," Altalune said calmly. She noticed the two girls exchange a glance before laughing.

"Us help you? Yeah right like we'd ever do that," The girl with choppy hair said gently, she snapped her fingers. Two men walked in, one picked up Calla who screamed in surprise while the other one quickly disarmed Ted and knocked him out before they both left the room carrying them with them.

"Hey! What are you doing!? Bring them back!" Altalune yelled binging her fists on the barrier.

"Don't worry we won't hurt them," The blond girl said. Laughing as they follow the boys out of the room.

"Dang it!" Altalune hit the barrier again then ran her fingers through her hair in frustration.

Staring at the door Altalune tried to come up with a way out but due to her lack of memories of this world she couldn't think of anything. She turned around to look at the girl still at the back of the cage, but found her asleep so she just sat there wide awake. She had no Idea how much time had passed but eventually the girl woke up.

Altalune got up, took her bag from her shoulder, and pulled out some of the food they packed before leaving and handed it to her. "My name is Altalune. Me and my friends are on a quest to get our memories back. We came here hoping the temple of Medea might have something to help us but now I see It's more like a hidden home for children of Hecate."

The girl stared at her then took the food and started eating. "The kids here won't help you, as you can see by the fact they locked me in a cage in my own room."

"Don't you have the same abilities?" Altalune asked.

"No Hecate is the goddess of many things not all her children will have the same abilities. I am best at Necromancy," she said as she slowly ate.

"Necromancy? Isn't that basically the same thing a child of Hades can do?" Altalune asked, thinking of Damon.

"Yeah, but I'm the only one who has this ability and I can't control it that's why they locked me up here. So I wouldn't cause any more trouble."

Altalune looked back at the door. "I know a child of Hades. He may be able to help you learn to control your abilities. I'll take you to him. If we can get out of here."

"What makes you think I'm going to trust you?" she asked suspiciously.

Before Altalune could respond the door to the room opened and the girl with dark skin and curly blond hair walked in carrying a tray with two bowls and two cups. "Breakfast." She sat the tray down and pushed it into the cage with her foot, which past the edge of the barrier.

Altalune didn't think she quickly grabbed her foot and yanked her inside, knocking over the tray causing the bright yellowish light of the barrier to shimmer again. "So the barrier is to keep people in not out. Well that was a dumb design now you're stuck in here with us."

"You are going to regret this. Eclair!" The girl yelled. A few minutes later. Eclair walked in.

"What is it Stacey?" Eclair froze in her tracks. "Are you stupid how could you get stuck in there?"

"This girl yanked me in!" Stacey snapped.

"For the love of Hecate." Eclair held her hand up and closed her eyes to focus.

Altalune quickly realized what she's going to do so she grabbed her bag and the girl's hand. Time seemed to slow when she looked back at the other two. Stacy was already pushing her hand through the barrier to make sure she could get through. Altalune knew that there was a small window to escape so she ran over and shoved Stacey, pulling the girl with her causing the three of them to stumble out of the barrier, crashing onto Eclair. Then she got up, grabbed the girl's hand again, pulled her out the door and ran down the hall.

"They Escaped!" Eclairs' voice yelled from the room as time went back to normal. The doors on either side of the hall opened up revealing a lot of kids.

Altalune didn't bother to count; she knew they were outnumbered so she just ran, squeezing the girl's hand to make sure they didn't get separated. When they reached the stairs, the room started to shake.

"They are trying to collapse the staircase so we can't get out!" The girl called over the shaking.

"Can they do that?" Altalune asked, looking back at all the children of Hecate.

"If they activate the defense mechanism they can," The girl said holding the walls for balance.

"Then go!" Altalune drew her sword. "I'll hold them off!"

"Don't be stupid you can't take them all."

"I have to try." She blocked the first sword attack then pushed him back before blocking the next.

There were way too many as she expected with each one she blocked, another gave her some sort of wound. She tried to move as fast as she could to try and see everything that was happening but she couldn't and she was starting to panic. The adrenaline rushing causing her to hear her own pulse pounding in her ears the room started to spin. The Hecate kids started to blur together; she couldn't even tell whether or not she was still moving. Then something happened the Hecate kids seemed to disappear then someone grabbed her hand.

They both start running up the dark and narrow staircase as it crumbled behind them and seemed to be closing in on them. When they reached the exit Altalune slipped as the last step fell from under her but she caught the edge of the bookcases and pulled herself out just as the bookshelves closed. Altalune just laid there on the floor, her eyes closed as she waited for the room to stop spinning and her heart to stop racing. Once calm enough she stood up and looking around she noticed she's alone. "Hey uh... Where did you go?" She walked around a bookshelf and found her pulling down a book. A few already in the crook of her arm. "We should really get going before your siblings get up here." The girl nodded and followed Altalune out the door.

Chapter 9

Apparently the Hecate kids decided instead of locking Ted and Calla up so they can't cause any more trouble they just kicked them out.

"Are you alright what happened down there? We felt an earthquake," Ted asked in a frantic worried tone when Altalune found them.

"I'm fine. Think we should rest for the day somewhere out of town," Altalune said letting out a shaky breath.

"Alright let's go find a spot in the forest," Ted said.

The six of them then headed into the forest and kept walking until they found a good place to camp out that was a safe distance from the town and near a river. Once set up Eleanor Altalune and Calla helped the new girl clean up and get into fresh clothes. "So um. What's your name?" Calla asked as she did her best to clean the dirty clothes.

"Calla don't. She'll tell us when she's ready," Altalune said brushing the girl's hair.

"No. It's Ok. My name is Rozlyn," she said.

"Well, It's Nice to meet you, Rozlyn. My Name is Calla. I'm a wizard, that's Eleanor and the girl brushing your hair is Altalune," Calla said chipperly as she hung the clothes.

"It's nice to meet all of you. Thank you for getting me out of there Altalune," Rozlyn said, turning to her.

"You're welcome." Altalune stared at her then gently uses the brush to part her bangs to the side revealing her golden eyes. She took a hair clip out of her own hair and put it in Rozlyn's hair. "Their now everyone can see your beautiful eyes."

Rozlyn stared at Altalune, her expression blank, then she grabbed a book from the pile she brought with her. "You mentioned that you and your friends are on a mission to get your memories back. Right?"

"Yeah why?" Altalune asked.

"There is a potion in here that might help. It's a potion of healing." Rozlyn then gave Altalune the book when she found the page.

Altalune read the page and stared in shock. "How are we going to get these ingredients? It's impossible."

"It must be possible if it's there," Rozlyn said.

"Can I see?" Calla asked. Then took the book when Altalune nodded. "What's Ichor?"

"It's god blood. It's gold instead of red," Altalune said.

"And what does 'bone of a virgin who dies of stress cardiomyopathy' mean?" Calla asked.

"Stress Cardiomyopathy is also known as a broken heart. It's a condition where emotional or physical stress causes rapid and severe heart muscle weakness," Rozlyn said.

"That's scary." Calla gave the book back to Altalune.

"Foods ready when you're ready to eat," Ted said, walking over from the direction of the camp, Rozlyn and Calla left first. Eleanor kissed him before following the others. Ted sighed as he looked down putting his hands in his pockets.

"Why do you love her?" Altalune asked once Eleanor was out of earshot.

"I don't anymore," Ted answered simply. "she's not the girl I fell in love with before."

"Then break up with her. I may not know you well but I do know this. You deserve better." Altalune walked past him and went back to camp. When she got there, she saw someone. "Damon."

Damon looked up from talking to Nick. "Hey," he said while he watched as Nick sat by the fire.

Altalune walked over. "Finally decided to come out of hiding."

"You knew?"

"That you were following us. Yes."

"I sensed a power similar to mine so I came to check it out," Damon said, looking at Rozlyn.

Altalune followed his gaze. "Ah. Well, it's a good thing you're here. I told her you could help her. We could also really use your help," she said looking back at him. "We need four ounces of crushed bone of a virgin who died of basically a heartbreak."

Damon looked back at Altalune like it was the most absurd thing he's ever heard. "Why would you need that?"

"It's for a healing potion. We think it could be the key to getting our memories back," Altalune said. "But it's ok if you don't want to. I know you like to be alone so we'll find another way by ourselves." Altalune took a step away from him but Damon grabbed her arm.

She looked at him, his gold eyes met her ocean blue ones for more than a few seconds. He then took his hand away again. "I'll see what I can do."

"What's with the change of heart?"

"I just decided to be helpful."

Altalune smiled softly "Fine. go ahead she could use your help learning to control her powers," She said then walked over to the group. "Rozlyn, are you ok with accompanying Damon to get the bone?" Rozlyn looked at Damon then nodded. "Thank you." Altalune looked at Ted as he sat down from coming back. "You are the only one who knows a dragon in this group so you need to figure out how to get a teaspoon of his tears."

"Um. What's a teaspoon?" Ted asked.

"One-sixteenth fluid ounces," Altalune replied but Ted still looks confused. Since he's never cooked or baked before.

"I think I can help him with that," Calla said. "I might even be able to use my magic. "

"Thank you, Calla. That just leaves Me, Nick, and Eleanor, to get a cup of Ichor" Altalune looked at them then sighed. *This is going to be fun.* She thought to herself. "Alright let's finish eating then get some sleep, we have a long day ahead of us."

"Who put you in charge?" Eleanor demanded. "Ted is the leader of this group."

"She found Rozlyn and rescued her. Without Rozlyn we wouldn't have the potion so I don't mind if she takes charge for a little bit," Ted said in Altalune's defense and the others agreed which clearly irritated Eleanor.

Once they were finished eating. Ted treated Altalune's wounds then they all went to sleep since it had taken the rest of the day to find their campsite. Altalune didn't realize just how tired she was until exhaustion took over. In her dream she was floating underwater and it was breathtaking. She could see the rays of sunlight as they shone through the surface. Below her feet the sand sparkled softly like someone sprinkled diamond dust on the sea floor. Suddenly a dolphin swam past her causing her to spin around revealing the moss covered rocks, the coral, the schools of fish, a hammerhead shark even swam to her gently brushing its body against her left hand then swam away as her body tensed in a moment of fear.

The dolphin from before chirped at her, grabbing her attention. It did a figure eight then swam away chirping happily. Altalune felt excitement rushing through her and she followed the dolphin catching up with it easily. They raced through the water dancing around with each other and simply having fun. Suddenly a dark shadow passed over them. Altalune stopped wondering what it was, the dolphin swam away along with the schools of fish that were nearby, looking around everything was fading into complete darkness. Panic started to rise inside her. Unsure of what's happening she tried to swim but she can't even tell whether she is moving or not.

She's about to scream for help when things get a little brighter. Now she's no longer in the ocean. Instead she's standing in a dark forest. In front of her was a spring shining in the moonlight. In the center was a small hill and on top of it was a small white flower bud looking like it's ready to burst open. She slowly approached the flower feeling as if she's being drawn to it but just as her finger was about to touch it, there's a flash of movement. She turned around and saw a dark figure then a bright green light shined so brightly she was blinded. Altalune woke up with a jolt panting then she looked down at her shaking hands.

"Hey, are you Ok?" Calla asked. Closing her backpack.

"Um. Yeah, I'm fine, it was just a dream," Altalune said, taking a deep breath to calm herself down.

"Demigod dreams aren't just dreams so I wouldn't take it so lightly," Damon said stretching.

"No one knows for sure if I'm a Demigod or not. So it could have just been a dream," Altalune said standing up.

"You are a demigod," Damon said firmly.

"How are you so sure?" Altalune asked getting annoyed.

"I can sense your power. Just like I sensed Rozlyn's and it brought me here. It's just a matter of finding out who your godly parent is," Damon said calmly.

Altalune started into the forest thinking of her dream, wondering what it could possibly mean. "Who cares, let's just get this over with."

I want to go home already," Eleanor complained, snapping her from her thoughts.

"First we need to find a clearing for Aiden to land in since I doubt the villagers would be happy seeing a dragon again," Ted said, shouldering his bag.

"I'll be taking Rozlyn to the underworld to teach her how to use her powers and find that bone you need," Damon said then put his hand on Rozlyn's shoulder and the two of them disappeared in the shadows.

"Alright then I guess we should start walking," Altalune said, and grabbed her bag.

"Walking where? How are we even going to find a god that'll be willing to give us some of their blood," Eleanor said sarcastically.

"Maybe I can send a prayer to Lord Hades and ask him?" Nick offered.

"You can try but even if he is willing, I doubt it'll be that easy," Altalune said and stared into the forest again. Just like in her dream she felt like she was being drawn somewhere but the pull was weak. "Let's go. Maybe we can find something that can help."

"Oh great idea, wander around aimlessly in an unfamiliar forest and risk getting killed," Eleanor said sarcastically but Altalune just started to walk ignoring her. Ted walked past Calla, Eleanor, and Nick to be by Altalune's side.

"Please tell me you have a plan that you've decided to hide from us," he whispered to her.

"Nope. I have no idea what I'm doing or where we're going, I'm just following my instincts," Altalune said not even looking at him.

"I'm all for going with your gut kind of thing but that isn't very reassuring," Ted said

"I don't know what else to tell you. We have nothing else to go on. So I guess you'll just have to trust me," Altalune said then stepped on a tree root before she jumped down.

Ted sighed and fell behind to stand next to Eleanor and Calla before the three of them continued to follow Altalune and Nick through the forest. They walked for a few hours before Eleanor started complaining. "My feet hurt. How long have we been walking?"

"It's only been few hours El," Ted said he looked up at the sky to determine the position of the sun but he couldn't pinpoint it through the trees.

"Can we take a break?" Eleanor whined.

"I could use one too," Nick said. "I've never walked this much before."

"What do you think?" Ted looked at Altalune but she was looking around with uncertainty. "Lu," he said louder to get her attention.

"Huh?" Altalune said, looking at him.

"Eleanor and Nick need a break," Ted told her.

"Yeah sure. Hey uh. Calla, could your magic help me climb the trees?" Altalune asked, staring up at a big tree in front of her.

"Yeah!" Calla closed her eyes and gently touched the tree Altalune was staring at. A purple aura surrounded her hand like it did before then it rippled through the tree. Then they all heard a female voice.

"Hey, hey, hey stop that, that's annoying!"

Calla jumped back from the tree confused. The trunk shimmered softly and a woman emerged from it. She had soft elf like features like pointy ears poking from her hair which was long and dark green like the needle of the tree itself, her skin was a dark brown like the tree trunk, her eyes were the same sunset yellow color of sap fresh from the tree, her dress looked like it was made from the pines of the tree itself. "Who are you?" Calla asked surprised.

"She's a tree Nymph," Altalune said in awe.

"Yes. My name is Ponderosa. What were you trying to do to me?" she asked looking at Calla.

"I-I was trying to make it easier for us to climb you," Calla said nervously.

"Climb me!? What do you think, I am your personal jungle gym?" Ponderosa clearly was not happy with the idea of being climbed.

"N-No Ma'am, I'm sorry Ma'am," Calla said nervously.

"Has anyone noticed this place smells like cookies?" Nick asked.

"That would be Ponderosa. When being warmed by the sun a Ponderosa pine can give off the smell of vanilla or butterscotch cookies," Ted said.

"Cool! Can we have some?" Nick asked.

"What would we need sticky icky pine sap for?" Eleanor said in disgust.

"Pine sap is a natural antibiotic! That has to be what the book means," Altalune said.

"I just thought it would taste as good as it smells," Nick said softly.

"What are you talking about?" Eleanor asked Altalune confused.

"Pine sap is a golden yellow color just like god's blood so whoever wrote this book might have been trying to keep the ingredients a secret as much as possible so he or she used code words that are similar to the ingredients but different enough so it isn't obvious," Altalune said.

"But what if that isn't the case? What if what's written is what we actually need?" Calla asked.

"Then we'll collect them both," Altalune said.

"Ugh! That's even more work to do," Eleanor complained.

"Yes, but there is no way of knowing which is the right ingredient until we test them out," Ted said and looked at Ponderosa bowing respectfully. "May we please use some of your sap for our healing potion?"

Chapter 10

Ponderosa stood there silently before softly nodding. "I will let you have some of my sap but only if you do something for me in return."

"We will do anything we can," Altalune said with a smile.

Ponderosa pointed to a tree next to her. "That's grandpa Douglas. At the top of his branches is a phoenix nest. The phoenix that made the nest has died and a new Phoenix will be reborn from the ashes at any minute now."

Calla gasped, "A baby phoenix!" she said excitedly.

"Yes," Ponderosa said. Her tone remaining calm.

"So what's the problem?" Altalune asked.

"I've personally grown attached to the phoenix before it was time for it to be reborn so attached that I can't help but worry about the little one's safety. So I would appreciate it if you would take care of it," Ponderosa said, looking at Altalune.

"Why us?"

"Because I know good people when I see them."

"I'll do my best," Altalune promised.

"But how are we going to get up there? My magic didn't work," Calla asked.

"It will. Just don't touch anything, just imagine what you want to do. Imagine your magic flowing through your body now. Hold out your hand. Your magic is flowing there pooling into your palm. Now release it, put it into what you want to create," Ponderosa instructed.

Calla did everything she's told and large vines grow and spiral around the Douglas fir. "Wow. How did I do that? That was so easy Before I would always struggle even though plants are my specialty."

"What many don't understand is the magic in wizards and the power in Demigods are different. A wizard's power stems from this energy in the world that no one understands. You can't see it, touch it, taste it, or smell it but when it's in a wizard's body they can feel its power and with training they can make it do and become whatever they want though most specialize in a single aspect. While a demigod's power comes from within. From the god they are decadent from, it flows through their blood. It's in their DNA. learn to hone it and control it," Ponderosa said.

"I have to relearn everything about magic," Calla said.

"You can practice later. I'm going to get the baby bird," Altalune said. "Ted can you get the sap?" She asked as she tossed him the spell book.

"Yeah, I'm on it," Ted said as he caught it.

With that Altalune climbed the vines and made her way up the tree she kept an eye out for a nest. Once at the top she poked her head through the leaves. The sun was blinding but once her eyes adjusted, she looked around. The sky was clear and in the distance, she saw the familiar pale orange scales of Aiden Ted's dragon friend, he was lying in a clearing of trees probably taking a nap.

She ducked back under and looked around for the nest carefully maneuvering through the entanglement of branches but when she found the nest she sat down and looked at the pile of ash. Thinking the baby hasn't been born yet. She sat there and waited.

"Looking for something?" A familiar voice said. Altalune looked in the direction it came from and she saw Stacey carefully balanced on one branch while hanging from another holding a tiny blue bird by its wing over the edge.

"Stacey No!" Altalune said in panic reaching for the baby. "Just hand it over."

"I think not." Stacey dropped it.

Without thinking Altalune jumped after it. A few seconds of falling later, she caught the baby in her left hand. She then held her right hand out and caught a branch but the force of her sudden stop caused her shoulder to pop out of place. Yelling in pain she let go of the branch and fell to one below her. She managed to land on her feet but since the branch wasn't very big, she almost slipped off as soon as she landed.

"That wasn't very smart," she scolded herself as she looked up wondering where Stacey came from and why she was trying to kill the baby bird. Then she looked down slowly, opened her hand. The baby phoenix actually looked like a full grown bird just smaller, about the size of a lovebird and its feathers were a beautiful metallic blue color. The scales on its legs, beak and talons were silver. Its eyes were like little sapphires. "Well, aren't you a pretty one. I didn't know a phoenix could be this color," she said and the baby phoenix simply chirped at her.

Altalune looked around to see where the vines were so she could get down again but she couldn't see them. Just her luck, now she had to climb her way down with a dislocated shoulder. Trying her best not to tear up from the pain she moved her left hand up to her left shoulder.

"Can you stay on my shoulder without falling?" she asked it unsure if it could understand her. It simply chirped before jumping onto her shoulder and perching in the crook of her neck. Once certain the baby wouldn't fall. She carefully jumps from branch to branch slowly making her way down.

"Where are you? I know you're alive." She heard Stacey's voice above her.

Groaning in pain and annoyance Altalune picked up the pace. When she got to the bottom, she found her friends in combat with Eclair and the two boys from before. Altalune tried to think of a way to escape safely but the pain was causing her head to spin and it was taking what little strength she has left to keep from falling over.

"Go," Ponderosa said. "I can slow them down just get out of here."

Altalune nodded. "We need to go now!" she called to her friends.

"Go where?" Ted asked while locking swords with one of the boys.

"That way." She pointed in the direction of the clearing she saw then leaned on the Douglas tree unable to stand up straight anymore. She watched with blurry vision as her friends broke free and started running where she said. The last thing she remembered was hunching over and throwing up as someone held her shoulders.

In her dream she was back at the spring in the middle of the forest, this time it was day and due to the sunlight, the water was so crystal clear, she could see the bottom was lined with stone and on some of the stones were the symbols of the gods some glowing brighter than others. Up on the little hill the flower bud was leaning over more than it was before making it clear it was dying. She reached out to try and touch it but remembered what happened last time she spun around just as something moved past her at blinding speed.

The next thing she saw wasn't there in the last dream. All her friends were fighting. The figure from before calmly walks towards her seemingly oblivious to the chaos around them. She still can't make out any features but it's clear that she has to fight it so she drew the sword Ted gave her and got ready for it to make the first move.

When she woke up the first thing she saw was the bright blue sky then Ted leaned over her.

"Hey. How are you feeling?" Ted asked.

"Like I just threw up," Altalune groaned and tried to sit up but she got an overwhelming pain in her right shoulder. "Ow!" She cursed.

"Easy." Ted helped her sit up. "We pooped your shoulder back into place but it's still going to be sore."

"Thanks." Altalune sighed. "Where's the baby phoenix?"

"Right here." Ted points to his lap. "It didn't want to leave your side. It seems to be attached to you."

The Phoenix jumped from Ted's lap flapping its wings a little and landed on Altalune's lap. "I think I'm going to name you Sapphire," Altalune said gently, petting its head with one finger.

"I wonder what you eat."

"Gems," Ted said. "She ate half the gems on one of Eleanor's bracelets."

"Maybe that's why she looks so shiny." She continued to pet her. "Where are the others?"

"Elenore is just sitting and waiting. Calla and Nick are collecting the tears of the dragon from Aiden."

"How?" Altalune asked.

"I talked to him. I asked him to think of something sad and Calla used some sort of spell. It sounds simple but it's taking hours to get enough tears," Ted said calmly.

"That's one ingredient down," Altalune said unenthusiastically. "Now we need god's blood."

"How are we supposed to do that?" Ted asked.

"That seems to be the million dollar question." Altalune carefully stood up, holding Sapphire in her hand before putting her on her shoulder as Calla walked over.

"It's done. One vial of dragon tears," Calla said, then gives Altalune the small vial of tears. Altalune takes it and holds it up. "It looks normal."

"Yes, but dragons aren't so there must be something special about the tears in order for it to be needed for the potion," Ted said.

"Yeah, you're right. Eleanor put this in your bag," Altalune said calmly.

Elenore looked up at her confused. "Why me?"

"Because out of all of us you'll be less likely to be caught in the middle of a fight all you do is hide behind Ted," Altalune said.

"Excuse me!?" Eleanor stood dropping her nail file. "I am not useless."

"You're in charge of protecting the ingredients. End of discussion," Altalune said and Eleanor snatched the vial from her.

"So now what do we do?" Nick asked as Altalune stared at the forest thinking about the dreams she had, feeling drawn like she did before but stronger. "We keep walking. I have an idea of where we are going this time. It's a spring with a white flower. I don't know why we need to go there but I do know that a fight is waiting for us when we do."

"Great, just what we need," Eleanor said, rolling her eyes.

"Should I scout ahead with Aiden?" Ted asked.

"No. I know how to get there." Altalune walked over to Aiden. She carefully reached her hand out and touched his snout. "Thank you for your help. We really appreciate it."

Aiden stared at her and didn't growl. He relaxed. He laid on the ground and let her pet him in a soothing way.

Chapter 11

She looked into Aidens eyes now that their eyes were almost level and just like before. She saw herself before she came into this world. The weak, timid, scared girl she truly is deep down. She closed her eyes and pushed that part of her aside.

She opened her eyes again she looked at her friends with determination. "Let's go," she said with confidence, she walked past Aiden and into the trees again.

Ted grabbed his bag, gave Aiden a pat on the nose in goodbye then ran to catch up with Altalune. "You certainly are confident."

"I have to be. If I doubt myself, we'll get nowhere," Altalune said not looking at him.

"Well it looks good on you." Ted smiled. "I'm glad you're taking the lead on this. Just don't go all emotionless on us."

Altalune giggled a little. "I won't. I promise."

"So how do you know where we're going?" Nick asked.

"It's hard to explain. It's this spring with a little hill in the middle and a white flower on top. It glows but it also looks like it's dying," Altalune explained

"Why would we need to go there?" Ted asked.

"I have no idea but we'll find out when we get there," Altalune said as they continued to walk. "How much sap did we get?"

"About three vials," Rozlyn said.

"That isn't much."

"Yeah, but it should be fine for the potion."

Altalune nodded in response then they walked in silence after that. Well mostly in silence. After about an hour Eleanor just wouldn't stop complaining, eventually she had Nick carrying her bag of useless items and Ted carrying her on his back.

"Ted, can we stop so we can cool off? It's soooo hot," Elenore whined.

Altalune clenched her hands into fists. Her patience towards the bratty wanna be princess is running low. "Will you just shut up! We'll take a break when we're all tired."

"But it's hot and my feet hurt!" Eleanor snapped.

Altalune stopped and turned so suddenly Ted stumbled back to avoid bumping into her. "Well maybe if you didn't wear heels!" she said, yanking them from Eleanor's feet. "To go on a mission! Maybe your feet wouldn't hurt so bad!"

"You better be careful with those they cost more than your whole outfit!" Eleanor snapped.

"Is it?" Altalune broke the heels off both shoes.

Eleanor screeched and squirmed. "How dare you! Those were a present from a prince!!"

"Yeah, a prince that wasn't me! Now stop squirming before I drop you!" Ted snaps. Eleanor fell silent. "Did you really have to do that?" Ted asked.

"Yes," Altalune said firmly. "She needs to realize the world doesn't revolve around her and not everyone is willing to put up with her stupidity." She dropped the shoes to the ground.

"How dare you say that! Do you have any idea who I am!? I can have your whole family stripped of their statice and thrown onto the streets like the filthy peasant you are!" Eleanor yells.

"Alright that's it," Ted said, his tone both annoyed and angry as he set Eleanor on her feet. "I am tired of you using my title to threaten people! You can't do those things just because you're my girlfriend and honestly I'm starting to question why I started dating you in the first place!"

Eleanor stared at him in shock then looked at Altalune again. "You did this! You turned my boyfriend against me!"

"No she didn't, you did this all on your own by being a mean selfish person!" Ted yelled.

Altalune gently put the hand of her good arm on his shoulder. "I get you're angry but you need to calm down."

"Oh like you breaking her heels is being calm," he said, shrugging her off. "If you don't start being nice to people, we are done," he told Eleanor then walked away from both of them.

Sapphire flew from Altalune's shoulder and landed on Ted's shoulder. "You can fly? You're only a day old?" he asked but Sapphire simply chirped.

"I think She's trying to comfort you," Altalune said walking over.

"I guess so." Ted gently pet sapphire's head. "Did you know she could fly?"

"If I did, my arm wouldn't be in a sling right now."

"Actually it takes about a few hours for a phoenix's instincts to fly to kick in," Calla said walking over. "Master Marco met a phoenix once. He spent a lot of time in the mountains studying it before opening the Rainbow Phoenix guild."

"I'm guessing he met a different colored Phoenix?" Ted asked.

"That's what he said but nobody believed him but me," Calla said smiling softly.

"When we get back, we can ask him more about it," Ted said gently, putting Sapphire back on Altalune's shoulder. Suddenly something caught his eye.

Damon and Rozlyn appeared from the shadows of a tree. Both of them look exhausted and like they just got out of a fight. Damon collapsed and Altalune caught him with the arm that wasn't hurting and slowly sat on him the ground.

"Damon, are you ok? What happened?" Altalune asked. Damon groaned and rolled so he's on his back, his head still in her lap. "Father seemed to be in a very grumpy mood today."

"He attacked you?" Nick asked.

"No. His soldiers did and they didn't hold back." Damon sat up slowly as he held his side.

"You're hurt!" Altalune said, a little panicked. "I don't know how to treat wounds."

"I can use my magic I know some small healing spells," Calla said as she sat down.

"After what the tree nymph told us about how your magic works, how will it heal people?" Nick asked.

"I don't know but I've done it for wounds before, so hopefully it'll still work," Calla said. She closed her eyes to concentrate her hands start to gently glow then Damon's wound starts to glow as well and he started to relax.

After a few minutes she opened her eyes again and the glowing stopped. "I only managed to stop the bleeding," Calla said.

"It's ok," Nick said, slipping off his backpack. "I've got bandages," he said as he opened up his bag.

"I'll help you," Ted said, walking further away from Eleanor.

Altalune watched as Ted and Nick wrapped Damon in bandages then did the same to Rozlyn once Calla was done using her magic. "So did you get the Bone?"

"No," Damon groaned.

"Great." Altalune sighed.

"After some rest. We'll go back."

"I'm coming with you this time," Altalune said firmly.

"You want to come to the underworld with me and Rozlyn?" Damon asked.

"Yes. I'm going with you this time for a little back up."

"What are the chances of me convincing you not to come with us?"

"Nonexistent."

Damon sighed. "What else do we need to get?"

"God's blood."

"Do you have a plan on how to get it?" Damon asked.

"Nope. All I know is where we need to go," Altalune said.

"And she's the only one who knows," Ted said. "What do we do while you're in the underworld."

"We can't do anything if she goes to the underworld," Nick said.

"Remember how we thought that the list of ingredients could have been codenames for what it actually was, you guys get those."

"Then let's go and get this over with," Damon said while he stood up.

"No. You need to stay here and rest first," Altalune said, looking up at him.

"If you can keep going with a hurt shoulder. Then I can keep going with this," Damon said as he looked at her arm.

"I will rest as well. We can leave tomorrow morning."

"Fine," Damon said stubbornly.

"I think I should stay here and read through the spell book to see what exactly needs to be done to make the potion," Rozlyn said.

"I can stay here with you," Nick offered. "I can take her back to the field with Aiden. That should be a good spot to stay with the space open. We'd be able to see anyone who tries to attack."

"That's a good Idea plus Aiden will be there. He can protect you," Ted said.

"I'm still going with Ted," Eleanor said.

"Fine but you're walking on your own with no complaining," Ted said sternly and Eleanor looked down at her bare feet.

Once everyone was ready after swapping certain supplies, they spent the rest of the day resting then that night went to sleep. In the morning they said their goodbyes and went their separate ways. Nick and Rozlyn went back to the meadow. Ted, Eleanor, and Calla went to find other ingredients. Altalune and Damon went to the underworld. Getting to the underworld was an easy thing for a child of Hades but with his wound and carrying Altalune, he collapsed as soon as they got there.

"Woe, easy." Altalune knelt next to him. "Are you alright?"

"Yeah, I'm fine," he groaned. "I just need a minute."

"Alright." Altalune stood and looked around. "So this is the underworld?"

"Yeah. Behind us is the river Styx. That building right there," he said pointing to a building a mile or so from them, "is the judgment pavilion. Or as I like to call it the courtroom. To the right are the fields of Asphodel. Above that was Elysium. To the left were the fields of punishment and all the way in the back; in between both, is my dad's palace where Cerberus plays guard dog."

Chapter 12

In the distance just like Damon said. Hades' palace stood higher than everything else. It was black marble and the blue fire light reflected off the Palace walls. "It's beautiful."

"Most people would find this place scary." Damon stood up.

"Well the faint screams from the fields of punishment are a little unsettling but the palace is beautiful."

Damon chuckled. "Well let's get going maybe I can talk to my dad see if he'll help us," he said as he started walking.

"So how often do you come here?" Altalune asked after a few minutes of awkward silence.

"A few times a week. I like to go to Elysium. Many people think Elysium is a place for demigods but it's not. I often see families reunited. They celebrate and have fun. They all look so happy."

"That's good."

They followed the lines of souls then walked past the Judgment pavilion. Before long they could hear Cerberus, then Cerberus tackled

Damon to the ground and all three of his heads were licking his face.

"Aaah Cerberus stop it! Down Girl! Down!" Damon tried to demand between his face being covered in licks. Altalune couldn't help but start laughing.

"Cerberus Down!" Damon managed firmly. Cerberus finally obeyed and got off of him. She sat down and watched Damon sit up. "Every single time I come by we go through this and every single time I end up soaked."

"Well at least you know she loves you."

"Tell that to the dog spit in my mouth."

"Well maybe instead of trying to order her to stop you should just let her lick you till she's tired," Altalune said as she walked over to Cerberus. She reached up and scratched the chin of the middle head. "Who's a good girl?"

Her tail started wagging happily as her heads started panting.

"Alright let's get inside so I can shower before we go see my dad."

"Alright," Altalune said, and followed Damon past the palace gates.

The gates were made of Obsidian and the palace looked to be made from black marble. Which explains why the blue fire light was reflecting off it so beautifully. "Hey, can you harness the blue fire?" Altalune asked him.

"I don't know, I've never tried," Damon said as he led her through Persephone's Garden.

Every plant they passed looked beautiful but deadly.

"So how many of these plants can kill me if I eat them?"

"Most of them and Don't eat the pomegranates you'll be stuck here forever."

"I don't like pomegranates anyway."

"Well when you're dying of starvation, you'll eat whatever you can find."

"Let's hope I never get to that point."

There were skeleton guards at the front doors. They nodded when they saw Damon then opened the doors for him. Walking inside the palace a cold chill ran down Altalune's back and an achy feeling settled at the base of her spine. She felt like someone was watching her, Following her every movement. Without even realizing it she grabbed Damon's arm and held on tightly. Not even noticing the dog saliva.

"Are you ok?" Damon asked, looking down at her.

"I feel like someone's watching me and I hate it when I feel like someone's watching me," Altalune replied as she looked around.

"Hey, you're fine. No one is going to hurt you here."

"I-I know. Let's keep going."

Damon nodded and kept leading the way. As they walked the torches lit up on their own. Revealing statues, paintings, more skeleton guards, and doors that only Hades knew where they led too. After what felt like hours Damon stopped at a door and walked in.

To Altalune's relief it was just a bedroom. It was simply decorated with a bed big enough to fit four people, a dresser, closet, bathroom, a very large TV bolted to the wall and a full size fridge.

"Woah," Altalune said in awe.

"Yeah, my dad's big on Simple yet not. It's strange," Damon said, grabbing a towel.

"No, I get it." Altalune said, opening the fridge. "Bourbon? Whisky? Rum? Are you even old enough to drink?"

"No. It was there when I first got the room. I won't touch it."

Altalune dug in the fridge some more. "Hey something healthy." Grabbed some fruit then closed the fridge. "Wait, can I even eat these?" she asked as she turned around. "Wow! Hey! a little warning please," she said covering her eyes since he took his shirt off.

Damon chuckled. "Well keep your eyes closed and yes those are safe."

"I am." Altalune didn't move her hand until she heard a door close and his muffled voice said it's all clear. She then sat on the bed and ate the fruit she found as she waited. An hour later he's walking out fully dressed with his towel on his head. "That was a long shower for a boy."

"Yeah, well getting Cerberus spit out of your hair is not easy."

"How's your wound? Do you need help bandaging it back up?"

"No. I already did it myself after my shower."

"So dog saliva AND treating your wound by yourself now an hour in the bathroom makes sense." Damon chuckled and tossed the towel into the laundry basket. "So why did your dad's skeletons attack you in the first place?"

"I have no idea. That's why I want to talk to him."

"Then we better get going." Altalune stood up and put what's left of the fruit back in his fridge then followed Damon back into the hall.

This time the feeling of being watched was softer but it didn't make her any less on edge. After a while it felt like they were lost but they eventually came to a set of large doors with torches on either side just like the front doors. The skeleton's there also nodded and opened the doors revealing the throne room.

The throne room was large and decorated just like the halls. The pillars had torches on them. Lining the left and right walls were rows of skeletons. At the far end of the room sat two thrones and in them sat Persephone and Hades. Persephone had light brown hair that flowed perfectly over her shoulders, her eyes were a dull mix of colors, and her robes were full of faded flower patterns. Hades has pale white skin and black eyes that sparkled like black ice on a road. His black robes flowed perfectly around him and shimmered like oil. His black hair was short and messy like Damon's.

Altalune felt fear rise within her. Then the familiar feeling of an anxiety attack rose within her. Her breathing became short and quick, as she started hyperventilating, her mind became cloudy, barely able to form a solid thought, she looked down at her hands and they were shaking so much if she tried to hold something she wouldn't have been able to. She knew if she didn't pull herself together, she'd be on her knees next. *Why now? Why is this happening now of all moments? Shouldn't this have happened when I got here? Is it the stress? Am I finally at my breaking point? Everything has been so strange and chaotic that maybe I haven't truly processed what's happening till now. Or have I finally lost my mind?* She looked back at Hades as he stared down at her. *This is his doing. This is his power.*

"Altalune what's wrong?" Damon said, as she crumbled to her knees but she could barely hear him. All her fears and insecurities came crashing down on her at once. She screamed as she hugged herself.

"What are you doing to her!" Damon yelled at his father.

"You know I can bring forth a person's greatest fear. She seems to have more than she can handle at once," Hades said in a smooth voice.

"Well make it stop, you know your power can make people die from their fear!"

"If she isn't strong enough to face her fears, she isn't strong enough for this mission," Hades said coldly.

Altalune collapsed. Passing out from lack of oxygen.

Chapter 13

Altalune gasped loudly and sat up quickly when she woke up.

"Easy you're ok now," Damon said gently brushing her hair from her face.

"What happened?" Altalune asked, looking around, Finding herself in Damon's room. "All I remember is having a panic attack."

"Dad was wearing his helm. He was testing you."

"Why? What did I do?"

"I don't know but you're lucky most don't survive the full power of the helm."

Altalune let out a shaky breath; she still felt weak from the experience. "Let's get the bone and get out of here. Who cares about your father's approval?"

"That's a dangerous thing to say."

Altalune stared at him with an expression that said she couldn't care less.

"Alright let's go." Damon led Altalune out of the palace and straight for the field of Asphodel. "Why here?" Altalune asked when Damon finally stopped.

"Just keep watch."

"Alright." Altalune looked around watching for skeleton warriors like the ones she saw in Hades' palace while Damon just stood there staring into the vast mass of souls wandering aimlessly and bumping into each other. Well actually they just went right through each other. Just like putting a drop of soap in a bowl of water and grease, the souls parted to the edges of the field. A single soul floated over to them.

"Good evening my lord, how may I help you?" The soul said.

"I'm assuming since you are the one who responded to me? you died-"

"Of heartbreak? Yes, I did," the girl interrupted. "You need the location of my grave, don't you?"

Altalune heard a snap. Like someone stepping on a twig she turned around and found an army of skeletons walking to them. "Um. Damon. You might want to hurry this along."

Damon spun around and cursed in a language Altalune didn't recognize yet she understood what he said. "Alright looks like we're taking this conversation on the run. Come on. Stay close behind me." Damon took the girl's hand and started running.

Altalune stayed on his heels. As they ran the souls parted before them and closed behind them. The Skeletons were running after them but from the looks of it, Skeletons running through a field of souls was like a person running through a lake that was deep enough for the water to go up to their hips. For the shorter skeletons it was even more difficult.

"Where are we going?" Altalune asked between breaths. "And I don't remember the field being this big when we walked past it earlier."

"That's because it's bigger on the inside than it is on the outside. As for where we're going. We're going back to the mortal world."

"Really?" asked the soul, Damon was dragging behind him.

Soon they saw the fence line and the river Styx Damon put his free hand on the fence and jumped over it.

Altalune did the same. "Why don't we just go out the way we came in?"

"I can't do that with the soul she'll get left behind."

"Then how are we getting out of here?"

"A secret tunnel."

They stopped at the river Styx. "There is no way we can jump that," the girl said.

Altalune stared at the polluted river. "What is this?"

"The hopes and dreams of those who died before getting what they wanted," Damon said.

Altalune knelt and tried to put her hand in the water. Damon grabbed her hand. "Don't your soul will be torn apart."

"Then what do we do?"

"I don't want to be torn part," the girl said. "Also those skeletons are catching up."

Damon sighed and put his hands on the ground. The ground started to shake and black rock started forming a bridge.

"That's cool," Altalune said when he was done.

"Yeah, well it's only temporary. Let's go."

They ran over the bridge and just as Altalune's foot hit the other side of the river bank the bridge crumbled. Altalune watched as skeletons tried to swim the river to get to them but were swept away by the current. She then turned and started following Damon again. He led them through the secret tunnel and they emerged into the forest. It was dark and raining. Altalune laid down on the grass and took a deep breath of fresh air.

"We should wait till morning. I feel like I'll collapse at any minute," Damon said as he leaned against the closest tree.

She looked at him and knew he was right; he clearly used too much of his power. "Ok. let's sleep."

Altalune and Damon were asleep in a matter of minutes. Altalune woke up to someone shaking her. She opened her eyes and found someone unfamiliar. He was cute in a scruffy way. His hair was a dark brown and his eyes were hazel.

"What are you guys doing out here?" he asked. "Have you been out in the rain?"

"Yeah," Altalune said, sitting up. "Who are you?"

"My name's Jett. I just came from Lamia."

"From where?" Altalune asked, confused.

"Lamia. The City of vampires," Damon said while studying Jett slowly. "How are you not dead?"

"Because me and the princess are friends," Jett said with a slight pause before friends. "She would never hurt me or let anyone else hurt me."

"Where is Lamia?" Altalune said curiously.

"See that large mountain?" Jett asked pointing to one that was very close to them. "The city is in there and it's beautiful."

"I'm sure it is but we have to go," Damon said looking around. "Hey where did you go?" He called into the woods.

"I'm right here." The girl's soul came out of hiding.

"It was nice to meet you Jett or whatever your name was but we need to get going. Come on Altalune."

"Hey if you're going back to the city, I can join you," Jett offered.

"We aren't going back to the city." Damon took Altalune hand and pulled her away from Jett.

"That was rude," Altalune said as she followed.

"We have a mission to finish."

"I know but you could have been nicer about it. Who knows maybe one day we'll need his help?"

"I doubt that let's get going."

After that they walked in silence. Which gave Altalune time to truly appreciate the beauty of the forest. Some trees were evergreens while most were trees that turn beautiful colors with the changing of the seasons. Altalune was so busy looking around that she didn't notice Damon had stopped until she bumped into him. "Ooops sorry."

"Shh," Damon said then pointed ahead of them. Standing a few feet away from them grazing on the grass was a Black unicorn. Its horn was like a long sword on its forehead and it sparkled softly like the night sky. The unicorn then lifted its head as four fairies flew around it. Suddenly a twig snapped. Altalune looked down and saw she had taken a step forward. Looking back up the unicorn was staring at her and the fairies were gone.

The unicorn slowly approached them. Damon carefully backed away but Altalune stayed still because just like her Pegasus. The unicorn was speaking to her in her mind.

"Who are you?" he asked her.

"My name is Altalune," she said her voice was surprisingly calm even to herself.

"Altalune," he said calmly. "Are you the one who gave my Mare her name?"

"Do you mean Aella?" Altalune asked. The Unicorn nodded gently, being sure he didn't hurt her with his horn. "Then yes. I am. I didn't know She had a… Boyfriend so to speak," Altalune said as she reached out to gently pet his mane. In doing so the fairies came out of hiding and flew around her making her giggle.

"From what Aella told me. You are on a mission," The unicorn said.

"Yes I am." Altalune holds out her finger and one of the fairies sits on it tilting her head as she stares at Altalune. She had brown skin, silver hair and storm gray eyes. Her wings were a transparent gray color with sparkling silver that made up the design of the wings and the more I studied her wings the more it seemed like the silver was moving like liquid silver. She was wearing one of those tavern waitress dresses from the medieval times. "We need to find something for a position that may be helpful on our quest."

"Let me give you a ride. It'll be faster that way."

"Are you sure? I really don't want to be a problem."

"I'm sure. Even your friend can join you."

"Thank you so much! Damon. We've got a ride!" Altalune said excitedly.

"And here I thought you were talking to yourself."

"Nope. I can understand horses. Now let's go." She sat on the unicorn after he knelt so it was easier for them to get on. After Damon was on. The unicorn stood up again.

"I'll lead the way," The girl said and soon they were off.

As the unicorn followed the girl. Altalune braided his mane. When they stopped, they were at the edge of the city. They had made it all the way back home.

"It seems we made it back home anyway," Altalune said. The unicorn walked straight through the city and everyone stopped and stared.

"Why is everyone staring at us?"

"Unicorns prefer to stay in the forest," Damon said. "They are seen often enough to know they are real but not so often that they are considered common."

"Oh." Once they reached the large cemetery Altalune and Damon hopped off the unicorn and followed the girl to her grave. "Your name was Kelly?"

"Yes. it was," Kelly said, sighing softly.

"Sorry about this Kelly," Damon said as he put his hand on her grassy grave. The ground started to break apart. Until a single bone was sticking out. Damon grabbed it and stood up. "Now let's just hope the others have everything else."

"Yeah, and the only thing that'll be left it will be the ichor."

"Let's head back." Damon and Altalune went back to the unicorn and got back on.

"We need to get back to our friends," Altalune said, petting his mane.

Chapter 14

"Think of them," he said in Altalune's head.

Altalune closed her eyes and did as she was told. Then she felt the unicorn start moving. She opened her eyes and saw the buildings and soon the trees flying past them as he ran. Ahead of them was a sparkly black transparent path leading through the forest. The unicorn's horn was glowing a dark bluish purple aura of magic.

The sun was setting by the time they slowed down to a walk and a few minutes after that they came to the clearing where Aiden was and the others were setting up camp for the night.

"I'll get a fire started," Calla said, putting her bag down, looking at Sapphire. "Do you want to help me?" She asked. Sapphire chirped and flew away. "Wait up!" Calla giggled and chased after her.

Ted started clearing a space for the sleeping bags.

"Hey guys we're back!" Altalune said. Damon jumped off the unicorn then helped Altalune down.

"Welcome back," Ted said. "Did you get what you needed?"

"Yeah. Did you?"

"Yes, we did, we got everything. All that's left is cooking everything which is Rozlyn's specialty," Ted said.

Rozlyn sat leaning against Aidan with a book in her lap, a few stacks of books around her as well as the ingredients. Damon gave her then bone. Then he and Altalune settled down to rest and clean up.

"I will be going," the unicorn said in Altalune's head. "Just think of me if you need my help."

"Ok. I will," Altalune said, then watched the unicorn leave.

"Hey, could you help me with this?" Damon said, trying to unwrap his bandage.

"Yeah sure." Altalune sat next to him and carefully unwrapped the bandages from Damon's side. Damon hissed in pain.

"This is really bad. What cut you?" Altalune asked.

"A rusty sword," Damon said, looking down at her.

"I need to clean this again. Eleanor, can I have the medical supplies you got from Nick please?" Altalune asked.

"Why should I?" Eleanor huffed.

"Just give her the supplies," Ted snapped. Eleanor did what he said, not wanting to make him angry anymore.

"Thanks." Altalune took out the supplies she needed. "This is going to hurt," she said poured what smelt like alcohol onto his wound using the rag to gently clean it. His whole body tensed but he didn't move. "I'm being as gentle as I can," she said.

"I know it's fine," Damon said, gritting his teeth.

"You really shouldn't clench your jaw like that, you could damage your teeth," Altalune said as she looked up at him.

"I'll be fine just focus on the stupid wound," Damon said in pain.

Altalune looked back at the wound as she poured more alcohol onto it. "I didn't know a wound could be stupid?" she said in a teasing tone.

"Whatever," Damon said in irritation but he was smiling softly at her. "So we have a baby Phoenix, dragon tears. Bone, sap from a tree, a few other ingredients and a group of angry Hecate kids after us," Damon said, summing everything up in a few simple words.

"Yup," Altalune said, now wrapping him back up. "You need a new shirt." She looked at Ted. "Do you have anything he can borrow?"

"Yeah, hold on," Ted said and opened up his bag he pulled out a black tank top. "Here."

Altalune took it and then went back to Damon. "So what's been going on?" she asked.

"Everything has been fine except for Eleanor being a royal pain," Ted said in annoyance. "Especially when it comes to feeding Sapphire."

Altalune sighed and closed her eyes. She thought about the dream she had where everyone was fighting around her. She didn't want to put her friends in any more danger. She already felt guilty because Damon got hurt. He would have been fine if she hadn't asked him to go to the underworld for her. If the others got hurt because of her, the guilt will only become stronger. She looked at her hand and it was shaking.

"Foods ready," Ted said as he walked over and gave a bowl to Damon and Altalune.

"Thanks," she said before slowly eating.

"Are you ok?" Ted asked.

"I'm fine," she said, staring at her food.

"Me and Rozlyn decided that. After you guys came back, we were going to split up again. Me, Eleanor and Calla would join you and Damon to find the Ichor," Ted said.

"Sounds like a plan," Altalune said but she had already decided once everyone was asleep, she would slip away. Whatever waited for them at the spring she would deal with by herself. She looked up at the sky and watched the stars slowly light up. Her plan could have worked but her body had a different plan, exhaustion washed over her and before long she quickly fell asleep. In the morning everyone was startled awake by a loud scream. Altalune was so startled she accidentally elbowed Damon in the side.

"Hey, I'm not the enemy!" Damon said, irritated.

"Sorry," Altalune said as she looked around. "What's going on?"

Ted and Calla were already up and dogging something that kept diving at them from the sky since it wasn't quite up enough for us to see very well. She then saw Sapphire her body ablaze in blue flames chasing after what looked like a bird made of bronze. As they flew around Sapphire's flames allowed them to see that there were more than one. It also helped that Aiden occasionally blew fire into the sky lighting up the entire meadow.

"What are those things?" Altalune asked as she moved to the side, making one of them hit the tree behind her but it was only stunted for a second before it came at her again.

"Stymphalian." Damon swung his sword at the bird that attacked Altalune since it was distracted by her; he managed to slice it in half making it crumble to dust.

"Stympha what?" she asked, then yelled in pain when another one scratched her left arm.

"Stymphalian," Ted said, protecting Eleanor from a bird diving to her head. "It's a bird that Ares created Right?" he asked.

"Yeah, apparently Hercules defeated them once," Damon said.

"Does anyone remember how he did that!?" Calla asked.

Altalune stopped to catch her breath. They were right, that's how the myth went but how did he do it? She then saw Eleanor who kept screaming every time one got near her. The sound seemed to be confusing the birds. "That's it! Hercules used a rattle given to him by Athena who got it from Hephaestus. Everyone stand near Eleanor and attack the birds that get disoriented if we take out enough of them the rest should leave!"

Everyone did when Altalune suggested. Eleanor didn't like that plan and screeched louder with each bird that came near them. After a while, the birds finally fled leaving the group panting.

"Who got hurt?" Ted asked.

"You," Nick replied noticing the gash on his shoulder from a bird's beak.

"It looks like we all need to be treated," Damon said.

"Of course Eleanor is unscathed," Altalune said rolling her eyes as she sat down.

"I got hurt, some of them pulled my hair out!" Eleanor yelled.

"How can you still yell after all that screaming?" Damon asked.

"Guys. I know we're all tired but the Stymphalian are coming back," Calla said watching sapphire circle the sky.

"We can't handle another attack from those things," Ted said.

"Then we run." Altalune stood. "Calla, can you use your healing magic?"

"No. I'm out of magic power."

"Then you and Eleanor pack up camp. Me and the boys will do a quick patch up on each other then one of us will treat you. Let's try and get this done before those stupid birds come back."

"Right." Calla went straight to work and for once Eleanor did the same without complaining.

Once everything was done. Altalune called Sapphire and the five of them ran off with as the flaming bird led the way. Leaving Rozlyn, Nick, and Aiden at the meadow. They ran for what seemed like forever jumping over roots and rocks, ducking under branches, and avoiding the attacks from the Stymphalian.

"I think we finally lost them," Ted said as they all slowed down. Then suddenly as Eleanor collapsed to the ground.

"Cyclops!" Altalune yelled.

They all jumped, barely avoiding its club smashing the ground causing a small crater. The impact caused the ground to shake, knocking

Calla off balance. "Where did that come from?" she asked as she got back up.

"I have no idea but there's two others behind it," Altalune said. "Let's just go!"

"Put me down! I want Teddy to carry me!" Eleanor complained. She was draped on Damon's shoulder which he had done to carry her out of the way of the cyclops' club.

"Hey if it weren't for me, you'd be dead so just be quiet," Damon said between breaths.

Ted fixed his pace so he was running next to Damon. "Are you sure you don't want me to take her? The wound on your side might open up."

"Yeah, I'm fine, she's actually lighter than she looks," Damon said and Ted couldn't help but smile.

"ARE YOU SAYING I LOOK FAT!!?" Eleanor screeched and squirmed.

"Yes, now stop squirming," Damon demanded and they kept running.

It seemed that no matter where they went, they would come across something else. A manticore, Minotaur and even a Chimera, finally they all collapsed, unable to run anymore all completely out of breath.

"We should be safe here," Altalune said as she panted.

"Are you sure about that?" Calla asked.

"Yeah. The monsters only showed up every time I tried to lead us to the spring. Right now I can tell where to go but it's far."

Ted groaned and laid back. "We've been running all day."

"I think it's best we rest up, properly treat our wounds and try again tomorrow."

"Sounds like a plan," Damon said and leaned against a rock closing his eyes.

"Do I really look fat?" Eleanor asked.

Damon looked at her. "No, your outfit is too much."

"What's wrong with this?" Eleanor looked down at her dress. Long in the back and short in the front her feet were dirty since Altalune broke her heels and she had anklets on both her ankles. At least five gold bracelets on each wrist, a necklace fit for a queen and a headband also of gold.

"We are on a mission. Didn't someone tell you to not dress like that?" Damon asked.

Ted raised his hand from where he was laying. "She doesn't listen to me."

"I thought the plan was to go to a town! I didn't expect to be running around the forest like this."

Ted sat up. "I told you when going on a mission from the gods things never go as planned!" He snapped at her. Eleanor hung her head then looked back at Damon "But without all this I'm hideous."

"Whoever told you that is stupid," Damon said. "You don't need a nice dress, fancy jewelry and a lot more makeup than you actually need to look pretty. Look at Lu Even covered in wounds and dirt with her clothes torn up she's still pretty. You want to be pretty, keep it simple. Also fix your attitude. You can be all dolled up as you want but what's truly ugly about you is your rudeness."

"Altalune is rude!" Eleanor pointed to her.

"Altalune is rude to those who are rude to her first. Haven't you noticed she treats the rest of us with kindness and care?" Ted said. "While you're standing here complaining she's been checking on everyone's wounds without even thinking about her own injuries."

Eleanor sat down and stared at her knees

"Will you guys stop talking like I'm someone special? I'm just doing what needs to be done," Altalune said calmly.

"You care about us, admit it," Damon said. Altalune simply kept working. "Here I can finish myself. Let Ted treat your wounds."

"No, I'm fine," Altalune insisted.

Damon took the bandage wrap from her and Ted took her hand and pulled her away.

Altalune thought about resisting but she was too tired to struggle. She sat against a tree and closed her eyes as Ted treated her. *They don't know me.* She thought. *They don't know who I truly am.* Memories of her true life flashed in her head.

All her life it was just her, her mother and her older brother who always protected her from bullies but eventually he left for college. She was always scared and timid, the bullies seemed to only pick on only her and she always struggled in school. Eventually she ended up turning off her emotions, she only cared about her mom.

Her only escape were the stories she read and her favorite shows to watch but since they were poor, she couldn't afford a library card or any form of T.V. She tried getting a job when she was old enough so she could help out and not ask her mom for things she wanted but she couldn't handle working at a fast pace and under pressure, she would always mess up and get yelled at and the yelling would trigger her anxiety. After losing her last job she met Rosaline.

Altalune was sitting in an alley crying because of what happened when Rose walked over. She had heard the crying and got curious. After Altalune explained she lost her job Rose took her hand and gently pulled her to an ice cream shop where they got ice cream and talked for hours quickly becoming friends. Who she was in this world was who she wished to be. Her friends trust her and she's been lying to them.

Next thing she knew she was dreaming. Altalune was standing on vibrant green grass that spread for as far as she could see all around her. While the sky was a starry night sky. She started walking, not sure where she was going and the more she walked, the more she could see she wasn't alone. Dragons were all around her but they were translucent as if they were simply dragon spirits. Some flew in the sky. Some were parents watching their children run around happily.

Then she came across three dragon spirits sitting in a circle. Staring down at what looked to be a hole in the grass. The one on her left blended in with the starry night sky and she only knew he was there because she could see his eyes and teeth when he opened his mouth. To her right was a dragon that started off as blue as the morning sky then faded into different shades of green into brown. The third dragon spirit sat across from her on the other side of the hole in the grass.

It was a soft salmon pink color that sparkled softly like dew drops on a rose petal. "I don't mean any disrespect to you but are you sure that this child was the right choice? Her insecurities may make it difficult to handle a mission like this." The starry Night dragon asked carefully.

"Her insecurities are exactly what's needed. This will keep her from getting a big head. As people like to say over there," The rose dragon said softly her voice sounded so familiar yet Altalune couldn't seem to remember why.

"What if she's so insecure she doesn't do a thing?"

"She will. With her heart and the realization that she has the power to do something she will definitely help anyone and everyone she can. Though all the power in the world won't help her persuade her fellow humans to change their ways."

"It will be hard," a new voice said, then a human walked from somewhere between the starry night dragon and the pink rose one. "But I know my granddaughter will be able to handle it. Especially with the help of her friends and her friends yet to come."

"And you're sure about this?" The earthy looking dragon asked.

"Yeah, humans aren't always right," The starry night dragoon said coldly.

"I am no mere human. I am a very powerful wizard and I know that her path may be hard but she will prevail."

"You may be confident but I'm still skeptical. We'll see what happens when the time comes" The starry night dragon said.

Then everything faded as she slowly woke up.

Chapter 15

She felt hands gently shaking her, she opened her eyes and saw Eleanor in front of her. "What the? What happened, what's wrong?" Altalune asked, looking around. She noticed it's just barely light out everyone else asleep around them.

"I-I was wondering if I could borrow some of your clothes? You have extra's right?" she asked.

"Yes. Mom packed an extra outfit just in case." Altalune said, confused. "What time is it?"

"Morning. I was hoping to change before the boys wake up."

Altalune stared at her. Then sighed slowly. "Alright I have two outfits. It's about time I changed as well so let's go," she said as she stood up and grabbed her bag. The two girls picked a spot and changed.

"How do you know what to do?" Elenore asked as Altalune braided her hair over her shoulder.

"Just because I don't spend hours in a shopping mall doesn't mean I don't know how to look nice."

"I'm sorry," Eleanor said softly.

"I know you are and the fact that you're trying helps."

Once done Altalune went back to camp with Eleanor behind her, Altalune wore dark blue jeans and a simple blue tank top with black boots, her hair pulled back in a ponytail. Calla and the boys were already awake when she got there and were cooking the last of the food over the fire.

"Hey Lu, where did you and Eleanor go?" Ted asked, being the first to notice her.

"We needed to change," Altalune said, setting her bag down.

Eleanor came from behind a tree and stood there nervously. "Well?" She was wearing blue jean shorts and a simple white blouse.

She wasn't wearing any makeup or jewelry and her long hair was braided with little flowers woven in the strands.

"See. Simple but beautiful," Damon said.

"I-I'm really sorry for the way I've been behaving. I promise I'll try to be better," Eleanor said.

Ted stood up and embraced her tightly. Eleanor cried into his chest. "There's the girl I fell in love with," he said as he lifted her face, wiped her tears, and gently kissed her. Altalune just sat next to Damon.

She stared at the grass in front of her thinking about her dream and the many questions that followed.

"Are you alright?" Damon asked

"Yeah, just thinking," Altalune said, keeping her eyes on the grass.

"Looks like your words and your clothes have changed Elenore for the better," Calla said.

"We'll see. No one can change overnight." Altalune grabbed some food.

"Why a white shirt?" Damon asked

"My mom picked it out and I don't argue with my mom," Altalune said.

"Ok. So what's the plan to get past the monsters?" Damon asked.

"We outthink and out run them," Altalune said.

"How?" Calla asked.

"We walk until we reach the first creature then I'll be the distraction while you guys run past. Then I find a way to get past myself and we keep running."

"No," Ted said, holding Eleanor's hand as he sits back in his spot. "I'll be the distraction. I'm the least injured and most skilled out of all of us, besides, you are the only one who knows where to go."

"Hey. I will admit to you being less injured but you are not the most skilled," Damon complained.

"I can't keep running if I know there's a chance one of you might not follow," Altalune said.

"But we can't go on without you," Eleanor said.

Ted looked at her. "The way you said that, makes it sound like we only care about her cuz she knows where to go."

"But she is the only who knows."

"Yes, but we also care about her because she's our friend." Ted looked at Altalune. "She's right though. If you die then there's a chance that so will the rest of us."

"I still can't bring myself to use one of you."

"I'll be a distraction," Damon said.

"What did I just say?" Altalune groaned in irritation.

"Hear me out Lu. I'm a child of Hades. I can travel through the darkness. If I'm the distraction I can keep the monster busy until you guys are out of sight then travel through the shadows of the tree to get back to you leaving the monster confused."

"That could actually work," Ted said.

"I could even use some of my magic to trap the monster while we escape," Calla said.

"That could work too," Eleanor said. "Meanwhile I'm useless."

"Don't worry about it. We'll keep you safe and we will get your memories back." Ted hugged her.

"I still don't know," Altalune said worriedly.

"We'll take turns," Calla suggested.

Altalune sighed there was no point in arguing about it anymore. They cared about her as much as she cared about them. "We'll decide who's the distraction depending on the monster we see first."

"That seems fair," Ted said. "We pack up and get going in thirty minutes."

Everyone nodded in agreement. They finish eating before packing up, like they planned. Staying alert in case of a surprise attack. Finally Altalune stopped walking and they heard the familiar sound of a lion's roar.

"Get down!" Altalune pushed Damon and Calla to the ground making all three of them fall while a spike flew over them. "We spread out. Make it harder for him to hit us all at once."

They all do what she said as the Manticore came into view. It watched them slowly spread out trying to decide which one to strike at first. "I can take this one," Calla said. "I can make a cage of vines to trap it."

"Are you sure that'll work?" Eleanor asked standing behind a tree.

"Yes," Calla said, her hands glowing a dark forest green.

"Alright," Ted said still slowly moving. "On the count of three. We all get behind it while Calla traps it." He looks at her. "Ready?" Calla nodded. "Three... Two...One."

Calla put her hands to the ground and used her magic to create a cage of plants trapping the

Manticore as everyone else ran. Except Altalune. She walked over slowly and put her hand on its nose.

"What are you doing!?" Ted yelled.

Altalune ignored him. The manticore tried to stab her with its tail but it was stuck in the vines so they just stared at each other, then the Manticore relaxed and stopped growling.

"Calla release him."

"But won't he attack?"

"No. Just let him go. Slowly."

Calla did as Altalune asked, leaving her and the Manticore standing there. Then Altalune gently started petting him like he was a normal cat. "There there. See we won't hurt you."

"It actually worked," Eleanor said, surprised.

"How?" Damon asked.

"I just showed him I wasn't a threat." Altalune smiled them giggled as the manticore laid down and dropped its head in her lap purring as she scratched his ears.

"I doubt the others will be that easy," Ted replied.

"I can still try," Altalune said. "Would you like to come with us?" she asked and the manticore roared softly. "Alright. let's go." She stood.

They kept walking following Altalune with the Manticore following behind the whole group, but it wasn't long before they came across the next monster. The Chimera jumped in front of them and breathed its fire, they dove aside to avoid it and Ted drew his sword. "I've got this one! Its fire is nothing compared to Aiden's."

"Put your sword away we aren't hurting them remember," Altalune said standing back up.

"I won't hurt it. I promise just go!" He avoided another fire attack.

Altalune looked around frantically. Trying to think of what to do this time. While Ted distracted it. Then she spotted something familiar. She grabbed some of the plant and ran to help Ted. He swung his sword and made it step back then she went close sliding in between them putting the plant under the lion's nose it froze its pupils dilated she meowed softly sank to the ground and rubbed her face on the plant.

"Catnip?" Ted asked looking at the plant.

"Just use it, it's better than hurting them."

"Snake!" Altalune called then put her arm in its way the snake bit her arm. She hissed in pain and dropped the catnip. Her attention wavered. She started playing with it, batting it back and forth. Slowly moving away from the group.

"Calla. Can you heal poison?" Ted asked.

"I can try," she said and rushed over to use her magic on Luna.

They all hear growling and see the Chimera and Manticore growling at each other over the catnip. "Play nice," Altalune ordered in a cat mother tone.

Their ears droop then they start playing together.

"Now what?" Damon asked, watching the two creatures.

"They might just help district the three cyclopes. Those guys aren't..." Ted trailed off.

"Trainable?" Eleanor asked.

"I was going to say they aren't much for seeing reason," Ted said. Then the Manticore growled and the Chimera and the Chimera growled back as the snake hissed again.

"Ey!" Altalune snapped her fingers. "Be nice both of you." She scolded them as if they were normal house cats. "Don't make me say it again." They glared at each other.

"Let's keep going." Altalune started running again.

Calla followed her while Damon and Ted looked at each other. Damon shrugged then ran after them and Ted sighed before following with Eleanor. Next was the Cyclops once again they jumped to avoid getting smashed by a club.

Ted had caught up in time to pull Elenore out of the way. "Wasn't there three of these guys."

"Yeah look," Eleanor said pointing. Sapphire was flying around one of Cyclops' heads as it was trying to swat her away.

"And there," Calla said.

"I can confuse these guys, just stay hidden till you can go ahead." Damon picked up a rock and threw it at one of the Cyclops blocking their path

"Hey Big guy over here!" The others hid as the cyclops turned his eye to Damon. "Come get me!" He ran in the way they came and the Cyclops followed him the Manticore and Chimera helped by biting and scratching the other two cyclops' getting their attention then following Damon.

Once it passed them. Altalune led the way again. After a couple minutes Damon appeared from the shadow of a tree and ran next to her and Sapphire was flying above her head. Before long it was quiet, too quiet. They stopped running to catch their breath but they stayed on high alert.

Altalune's mind was foggy. She was dizzy from the heat and tired from everything that has happened, not to mention whatever has been drawing her to their destination was close.

The pull was so strong she felt like she'd fall over if she wasn't careful or maybe that was just her being weak from running. Then they heard the familiar sound of a bull charging. The Minotaur came out of the trees, they just barely managed to dodge it leaving him to hit a tree.

"I've got this," she said standing.

"Are you sure you can handle this on your own?" Ted asked her.

"Yes, just go." Altalune watched as the Minotaur turned his attention to her. "That's it, look at me big guy." The Manticore and Chimera get ready to attack. "Hey." She snapped her fingers at them but this time it doesn't seem like they are listening.

The Minotaur charged again and Altalune dove out of the way again. The Manticore and Chimera attacked but they were quickly thrown to the side. When he turned his attention to Altalune again. she grabbed her sword and threw it aside out of reach. His eyes follow it then look back at her as he gets ready to charge again.

"Are you crazy!?" Damon yelled from where they were waiting for her to catch up. He grabbed his sword but before he could pull it all the way out Ted put his hand on his arm. "Why are you stopping me? She's going to get herself killed!"

"She told us she can handle it so let's trust her especially after what we saw with the Manticore and Chimera," Ted said not taking his eyes off Altalune and the Minotaur.

Damon looks at Altalune worried about her hoping she'll be fine. He pushed his sword back in its sheath and the sound made the Minotaur look at the group but before he could charge at them.

"Asterius," Altalune said gently and he looked at her. "Hi," she said softly, gently holding her hand out as she looked up at him. "You don't have to do this. I know you are angry but we aren't the people you're mad at. Don't take out your anger out on us when it's that stupid king's fault. He made Poseidon angry. Poseidon chose to punish him and you are the result." She watched as the Minotaur slowly sat down.

"He didn't even give you a chance. Maybe you could have been something great if you had the love and care you deserve. As well as learning to embrace both human and bull. I want to give you that chance. It's not going to be easy but maybe you'll be happy in the end."

The Minotaur. Asterius hung his head. Altalune smiled and gently put her hand on his forehead. "You would like that wouldn't you? You want to be happy. If you can help me by letting me pass with my friends, I promise we'll come back and take you to school with us. There you can learn everything you need to."

Asterius nodded slowly.

"Thank you." Altalune walked to the Manticore Chimera to make sure they are ok then went to her friends.

"How did you do that?" Damon asked.

"If you were born with some sort of problem, wouldn't you want someone to just accept you and help you?" Altalune asked, knowing that anyone could be an outcast. "The world is cruel with people shutting others out or hurting others for being different. I don't want to be that way." Sapphire landed on Altalune and gently rubs her head on her chin. Altalune giggled and gently petted her head. "I guess you agree."

"We all agree with you," Eleanor said. "At least I can speak for Teddy since I know him so well." Ted nodded in agreement.

"I agree to," Calla said.

"You are insane for attempting something like that," Damon said, "for attempting all of it." He looked at the Manticore and Chimera. "But I'm glad you're ok."

Altalune smiled a little "Let's go. We are close." She led the way.

Chapter 16

As they got closer she became hesitant she knew going there would lead to a big fight but they had no choice. She just hopped that everyone would be ok and no one would be too hurt. Though they have something she didn't have in her dreams. Asterius, the Manticore and the Chimera. Maybe they could give them the advantage they needed. Even though she did not want to make them fight for her.

Before long, the trees thinned revealing a small clearing. In the center was a small spring with a hill. On that hill was a little white flower still wilting but also glowing.

"Wow. This place is beautiful," Elenore said in awe.

"It feels magical," Calla muttered also in awe.

They heard a roar that shook the air around them. "Aiden!" Ted said happily as he looked up at the sky and sure enough Aiden was approaching. There was just enough room for him to land and for Rozlyn and Nick to slide off his back.

"Is this the place?" Rozlyn asked.

"Yeah, it is," Altalune said.

"This place is awesome," Nick said.

"It's done all we just-" Rozlyn started but was interrupted by a familiar voice.

"Thank you for finishing the potion for us," Eclair said giggling as she approached from the way they came.

"And thanks for dealing with the monsters for us," Stacy said. "I was impressed at how you managed to tame them. Too bad we had to kill the Manticore and Chimera."

Just then some of their siblings came from the woods behind them and tossed four decapitated heads in between the groups. Elenore screamed and ran to hide behind Aiden. Damon and Ted drew their swords. Calla got ready to use her magic. Rozlyn used her necromancing skills to summon some skeletons and little Nick picked up a big stick.

Altalune felt nausea build up in the back of her throat and she watched as war broke out before her. She knew what had to happen next. She went to the spring. Looking down in the crystal clear water she saw the symbols of 14 gods all shining but one symbol was the brightest. The trident then like in her dream she felt something behind her. She spun back around. Standing before her was a man at least 12 feet tall. He was dressed like a normal fisherman and smelt like it too with the scruffy beard and everything but his sea green eyes made it clear he was NOT a normal fisherman.

"Poseidon," she mumbled.

Something about the sea god felt familiar, almost comforting but she knew he wasn't here to talk. Altalune drew her sword. Without thinking without having a plan she just started swinging her sword. She knew she couldn't kill him but all she needed was to make him bleed. However, doing that was easier said than done. She fought like she had been fighting for years but every time she gets close to drawing blood, he fizzes into nothingness then materializes into a different spot further away from her.

"Stop running from me you coward!!" She snapped as she stopped to catch her breath. She then noticed her friends behind him. They were losing the battle since there were more Hecate kids trickling out of the forest like a stream. She looked back at Poseidon then ran past him to help her friends. Just before she could reach any of them, one of the Hecate sons stabbed his sword through Damons side. The same side that already had a slice wound from one of his father's skeleton soldiers. Damon collapsed.

Altalune froze, then she heard a scream. Following it she saw Eleanor being dragged by her hair. Nick was being held off the ground. Ted was on one knee a dagger in his shoulder and his sword out of his reach. Rozlyn was pinned to a tree with a sword at her throat. Calla was surrounded, she was panting heavily, clearly sweating and her magic was flickering like a light bulb about to die. Even Asterius was being overwhelmed.

Despair rose inside her. Everything she wanted to avoid was happening. Overwhelmed she collapsed to her knees screaming loud enough to be heard over the roar of battle. The water from the spring shot into the sky like a geyser then it rained down on everyone in the little meadow.

Everyone stopped fighting and watched in shock. Altalune found her strength again thanks to the water and stood up. She stood there seemingly calm. "Get her!" Eclair screamed.

Everyone on her side ran to Altalune. She just smiled. The water trapped each and every one of them by their feet causing them to face plants on the ground. They struggled to get free but couldn't.

Altalune calmly walked past them and gently took Damon into her arms and rested his head in her lap. Damon simply groaned in pain. Water surrounded her hand and she held it over his wound.

"Rozlyn give it to them."

"But It's-"

"It's not worth it. Just do it."

Altalune looked up and met Rozlyn's eyes. Realization dawned on Rozlyn's face then she took the glass bottle from her bag and gave it to

Eclair. "Wise choice." Eclair took the bottle. "No set the others free."

The water sank away from them and they all left. It was silent for a few minutes before Altalune spoke again.

"Nick. Treat Damon's wound as best as you can. I managed to stop the bleeding." She stood and grabbed Damon's sword. It was heavier than it looked but she didn't care. She faced Poseidon, who had been standing there watching silently "I'll try to get the gods blood," she said as she took an unsteady step forward.

"That won't be necessary. I have no intention to fight my daughter any longer," Poseidon said as his form changed to something more human. Meaning he became the height of an average male adult then he walked over to her. He gently took the sword from her hand and used it to slice the palm of his hand. "Does anyone have something I can put this in?"

Rozlyn frantically dug in her bag and pulled out an empty glass bottle. Poseidon took it and tilted his hand letting his golden blood drip into the bottle. After a few minutes he gave it back. "Is that enough?"

"Yes, this is plenty." Rozlyn smiled. "Now I can finish the real potion."

"Why did you just give it to us?" Ted asked.

"Like I said, I have no intention of fighting my daughter," Poseidon said. "I think you have more than proven yourself."

Altalune just stared at him, having trouble processing it. He was her father. Even in the real world she didn't know what it was like to have a father. He left before she was old enough to remember him, now, she stood before her dad in this magic world and he is a god. She didn't know what to think or how to feel. She was physically, emotionally, and mentally tired. Her wounds burned, her legs screamed at her not wanting to hold her weight anymore. It took what little strength she had left to just walk up a tree and sit down.

Sapphire landed on her shoulder Asterius curled next to her. Losing herself in her thoughts. The exhaustion was still overwhelming but the pain made sleep hard. She didn't realize how late it had gotten until cold air swept past her making her shiver. The moon lit up the meadow the stars sparkled like gems in a cave. Everyone else was asleep except Rozlynn and Poseidon. Altalune carefully got up her body screaming at her and went over to where Rozlynn was putting the potion in bottles.

"Is it ready?" Altalune asked.

"Yeah it is." Rozlynn gave her a bottle. "This should heal anything from minor wounds to deadly sicknesses."

Altalune took it. The bottle itself was made of a dark glass but even so, it glowed like liquid gold. She went to Damon, gently propped him up and trickled a little of the potion into his mouth. She looked down at his side and watched as the wound started to heal. She set his head back on her backpack then went to the others. One by one giving them some potion. By the time she was done everyone was awake and feeling much better.

She then took the second bottle and went to the spring. She was moving slowly because of how much pain and exhaustion she felt, but when her feet hit the water, she started to feel better. It was freezing but pleasant. She sank to her knees. The water covering her waist. She poured the potion in the water and watched as it spread throughout the whole spring then was absorbed into the little hill like veins of gold.

It healed the flower. Standing up straight, the flower bloomed, releasing tiny glowing orbs that flew around most left the meadow. While four stayed. One flew to Eleanor, the other to Calla, one to Nick and the final one to Altalune.

Chapter 17

Memories flooded her mind of her life here. She was a happy child, carefree and creative but also brave. She stood up to any bullies and she was a great student. She had her flaws, mistakes she's made, things she felt guilty for, but no one is absolutely perfect. The wind blew again and suddenly she felt eyes all around her.

She looked and saw creatures emerging from the forest. An eagle, a peacock, a black ram, a cat, a fox, a deer, an owl, a crane, a vulture, a swan, a leopard, a pig, and a bunny. Then all those creatures turned into the gods. Zeus, Hera, Hades, Hestia, Apollo, Artemis, Athena, Hephaestus, Ares, Aphrodite, Dionysus, Demeter, and Hermes.

All her friends bowed. Even Aiden the dragon seemed nervous and Altalune was too. Thirteen gods plus Poseidon made fourteen all in one place. That couldn't be good. Altalune wanted to bow but she knew if she tried, she'd fall flat on her face. That and she was comfortable sitting in the water. She remembered something about how the gods choose how they liked to appear, so Zeus being a short chubby man like Dionysus was surprising.

At least she was assuming he was Zeus since he was the one that changed from the Eagle. The rest looked like they fit for who they are. Well in Altalune's opinion.

"See I told you my daughter was the one," Poseidon said.

"There's no need to brag," Hera said as she walked over to Altalune. "You have passed the test." She had black hair and soft brown eyes. She was wearing a long dress made of Peacock feathers.

"Past what test?" Altalune asked.

"We needed to find the right person to go on an important quest and that person is you. You are strong, brave, tactful and kind. You tamed the Minotaur and gave him a chance at a better life," Hera said, glancing over at Asterius. "You treated your friends first and made sure they were ok before healing the flower to finish the mission without even thinking about healing yourself. You are what we need."

Apollo walked over smiling. He looked like he did in the holographic scroll image, short messy golden blonde hair, and eyes as blue as the morning sky. He looked no older than nineteen. "This is where I tell you the bigger prophecy.

Descended of wizards,
Child of a god,

Favored by the wise,
A journey with solutions you must devise.
When seven keys shall be made one,
A door to another will be undone,
A mystical land is what will be found.
Forthwith a world in chains shall be unbound.

He then touched her forehead and all her pain and exhaustion just melted away. Then he returned to the line of gods.

"You may choose others to join you if you wish or you can travel alone."

One by one each god faded. "We are counting on you." Hera was the last one to fade leaving the group alone again.

Altalune sat there trying to process what just happened. Ted walked over. "We should get going. You need time to process this."

"Yeah sure." Altalune followed him to Aiden and they flew back home. Asterius followed below them.

They got back to the city a few hours before school started and each went home to freshen up and get some food. When Altalune walked in her home her mom smothered her in a hug causing Sapphire to jump on her head. Once free, Altalune told her about her adventures, her memories coming back and that she has to go on a new mission while having breakfast. Understandably her mom looked worried but she supported her anyway. Afterwards she went to school.

The group surrounded Asterius, Altalune and Ted taking the lead and went to the headmaster ignoring the shocked looks on the way. They explained everything to him and Headmaster Charles accepted Rozlynn, Calla and Asterius into the school.

"Now Altalune," Charles said carefully as they walked with Asterius. "It won't be easy for the Min- I mean Asterius. It won't be easy for him to fit in and the trauma he's suffered is..." he trailed off.

"I know, headmaster but we have to try. He deserves to be happy."

"Are you sure this will make him happy?"

"We won't know until we try."

Altalune and the headmaster took Asterius to an empty classroom and spent some time trying to teach him the basics. Asterius' short temper proved to be a challenge but they kept trying.

Afterward Altalune had a lot more to do. She had to get back into her daily schedule. She had to meet and get to know her siblings, other children of Poseidon, and do some research for her next quest. On top of all that, any spare time she had in between was spent helping her friends. Like helping Eleanor pick a whole new simpler wardrobe. Helping Calla with her Magic studies. Damon, Rozlynn, and Nick didn't need her as they helped each other and bonded but she'd still check on them anyway.

Then there was Ted.

His father had announced that there would be a huge party in celebration of the quest being completed. Ted was in charge of planning the whole thing but since Ted felt that Altalune was the main guest of honor so the party should be decorated the way she likes. While Altalune thought it should be decorated for everyone. There was a lot of arguing. By the end of two weeks, it's the day of the party and she was more than stressed.

Standing in the large ballroom, she was having the guards rearrange the tables for the sixth time.

"How are things in here?" Ted asked.

"Buffet table. Dessert table. Then the seating tables like this. Leaving all this for dancing."

"That looks good, where's the table for presents?"

"We don't need presents."

Ted sighs. "Get a table over there for the presents please," he said point by one of the doors.

"I really think the others should be here. I'm not the only reason the quest went well."

"I know you're not the only guest of honor, but you were the leader of the group. Without you would have had no idea where that spring was."

"And you know I have no idea how to plan an elegant party? Children's parties are easy. This, nope."

Ted gives her a clipboard. "Just finalize stuff."

Altalune looks at it and the first list is the main meal. She takes the quill and crosses out the entire seafood section. "Unless you want me throwing up during the party then no." She looked at the side dishes. "I like some of these, the others I can just avoid." She looked at the desserts, crossed out the coconut. "No." Crossed out the grape. "Unless it's fresh and green, no." She looked at the beverages. "Coffee I can handle just won't drink. Not a big fan of tea except raspberry," she said, circling it. "But keep other flavor options for others and keep extra sugar on the side. I like my tea sweet but others might not. Again for the juices no grape." Crossed it out. Look at the tablecloth choices. "I like this one. And keep the room dim, not too bright and the music is fine." Give him back the clipboard. "Was that helpful enough?"

"Perfect see you tonight." Ted walked away.

Altalune sighed and left the room only to run into Eleanor, "Can you help me pick a dress for tonight please!"

"I thought you already had your dress planned?"

"Please Lun I'm panicking here!"
"Ok. Ok."

Eleanor took her hand and pulled her to one of the guest rooms in the palace that she usually stays in and showed her all of the dresses laying around. "Woah! What happened to that nice pink dress you chose?"

"It's right here but it's not perfect enough."

"El it's great, it's a simple beautiful light pink color that gives off this lovely springtime feeling especially with your green eyes. With the white flower pattern scarf over your shoulders and the light pink jewelry set that matches. it's perfect."

"But what if it's not… what if Ted doesn't like it? What if my dress gets ruined at the party? I need a backup."

Altalune grabbed her shoulders. "El, calm down. I'll help you pick out one back up, then that's it. Your dresses go back in your closet and don't come back out until it's time to wear them."

"Ok thank you." Eleanor hugged Altalune. Then they started planning outfits.

Chapter 18

It took hours for Eleanor to finally settle on a second outfit she liked so by the time they were done there was only a few hours before the party left. Altalune walked out of the palace and walked home. She spent an hour grooming and feeding Aella. Then she went inside and spent some time playing with her cat. Then went to her room and found Sapphire eating the gems off one of her bracelets. In just two weeks she had grown to the size of a hawk.

"You're going to eat all the gems in the house, aren't you?" Altalune asked her as she gently pet her feathers. Sapphire cooed and rubbed her head against her hand.

She spent the next hour getting ready. She chose a dress that started off black and faded into blue. It is short in the front but also long and flowy in the back. She wore simple knee high heeled boots. Her hair was half up half down and wore simple jewelry to match.

When she arrived in the ballroom she was guided towards the front where everyone else was standing. Ted's dad had made a big speech and everyone cheered at their accomplishment but She could barely hear a thing. She was trying to find the table she had put in a specific spot in a corner so she could hide. She hated being the center of attention. As soon as she could get away, she went straight for her corner but couldn't find her table. Ted must have moved it. Groaning in annoyance she walked to the desert table and spent most of her time there. That is until Damon walked over.

"Looks like someone has been hiding in the shadows," he said in an amused tone.

"Amusing coming from a Child of Hades."

"At least I'm socializing."

"I don't like big crowds and I don't know anyone here except you guys."

Damon chuckled and offered his hand. "May I have this dance?"

"You dance?" she asked.

"You won't know until you see for yourself."

She smiled softly and took his hand. He smiled back and swept her towards the middle of the dance floor.

"I'm not a good dancer." She warned as he held her close.

"That's fine. We won't do anything complicated."

"No. It's fine. Test me. We can see how much we know."

Damon smiled. "Are you sure?"

"Are you scared?" she asked in a teasing tone.

"Of course not." He led her to the dance floor.

The next song starts and the dance to it, moving gracefully and perfectly in sink. Taking up the entire dance floor, leaving everyone in awe.

"I thought you said you weren't a good dancer?" Damon asked.

"I think I'm not a good dancer. Others' opinion may be different."

Damon lifted her up and spun her around before slowly setting her down again. "So why aren't you wearing shoes?" he asked.

"I took them off somewhere."

"Why would you take your shoes off in the middle of a party?"

"Because I felt like it. Where did you learn to dance?"

"My mom used to say the best way to a woman's heart is through the dance floor."

"Music works too. I love music."

"I'll keep that in mind." They danced in silence for a few minutes. "So when are you leaving?" He asked.

"I don't know. Maybe during winter break. Maybe sooner the only part of the prophecy that sort of gives me a clue is the seven keys shall be one part. I'm assuming it has to do with the six major kingdoms of six different creatures representing six different elements but it said seven so I have no idea what the seventh is."

"That makes sense. Sort of. Who are you going to take with you?"

"Calla. She wants to learn many different kinds of magic and this is the best way for her to do so."

"Let me come with you."

Altalune pulled back and looked at him. "Why?"

"Well you said six creatures representing six elements, right? Well the demon kingdom is in the underworld just past the pit that leads to Tartarus. The fastest way to get to the underworld is to travel using one of my abilities, the other fastest way is to die."

"You make a very good point. Alright, you can come."

Damon chuckled as he dipped her then slowly pulled her back up. Altalune giggled then led him off the dance floor and out the balcony doors. She leaned against the railing and took a deep breath of cold fresh air. "The nighttime is relaxing when you're not in a lot of pain and running from monsters."

"Yeah it is." Damon gently wrapped an arm around her back. "How's your shoulder?"

"Perfect. I guess that's what happens when the god of medicine heals you. How's your side?"

"There's a small scar but all I got was a potion made of god's blood."

"Hey. I didn't ask Apollo to heal me."

Damon chuckled. "I know."

"When you think about it. Our little world of gods and monsters is small. There is so much more out there. Wizard, Demons, Angels, Vampires, Elves, Fairies, mermaids. I have a feeling we'll meet them all on our quest. Maybe even creatures we don't know exist, other types of gods too."

"You do know if we do most of them will be hostile."

"I know but I want to befriend all of them."

"I don't think I've ever met anyone that wanted to befriend the other races."

"Well I'm different."

"And different is good. Maybe it'll actually help us."

Altalune giggled softly. "I may not be able to make a change at home but maybe I can make a difference here." She mumbled softly.

"What did you say?"

"Nothing, never mind." She turned to him gently and put her hands on his chest. "Tell me about your mom."

Damon sighed softly. He glanced away before looking up at her again. "She's gone. So are my sisters. They were killed. I watched it happen. I would have been angry but I saw that there was pure guilt and fear on her face. I don't think she meant to do any of that and she looked scared of what she is."

"Did you know her?"

"No. She could have been possessed or something."

"If I can, I want to help her to if I can."

Damon pulled her close. "You can't help everyone in the world."

"I can try."

"You're too pure. Too innocent."

"That's not a bad thing."

"Let's get back to dancing."

"Lead the way prince of death—"

"Don't start—" Damon said gently, pulling her back to the dance floor. "Hey what if we started a food fight instead?" He asked her.

"That sounds even better," Altalune said in excitement. "Just don't hit Eleanor."

"Duh. I'm not an idiot." He chuckled.

Both of them grabbed trays of food and with a mighty battle cry from Damon the elegant party turned into the best and only food fight war the palace has ever seen.

Chapter 19

After the party everyone went back to their daily grind. Altalune's schedule was so packed she decided to stop visiting her friends all the time and just focus on the most important things. School, training, and research. Except there's only so much a book can teach you and it was likely the things she was reading weren't true. Eventually she gave up on the research and started focusing on just school and training, accepting the fact that the best she can do is prepare herself as much as she can before the long trip ahead of her.

Three days before the day she and her friends will be leaving. Altalune was in the gym brushing up on her sword training with her siblings. She had four of her brothers surrounding her at once while the others watched. It wasn't easy but she eventually took them down one by one. The last to fall was the eldest of the family, Lucas. She knocked his sword from his hands, made him trip, then pointed her sword at his neck. They stayed like that for a few seconds staring at each other before he burst out laughing.

"You were always the strongest in the family," Lucas said.

Altalune backed up, still panting a little as she held out her hand and helped him up. Suddenly the gym doors burst open and Ted walked in.

"Ted dude. I know you're the prince but it's our time for the gym," Mike, her second eldest brother said.

"I need to train now," Ted said as he walked across the gym. Taking off his blazer. His voice was filled with rage. He hung his blazer, tie, and white button up shirt leaving him in just a white tank top. He grabbed his sword and turned to Altalune's demigod family.

They looked at each other, half of them confused and the other excited. One by one they approached Ted and soon a fight had started. Except the fight was very one sided.

Ted was stronger than all of them and it was clear he was not holding back. Lucas held out for longer than the rest but soon only Altalune was left standing against Ted.

"What's wrong?" she asked softly. "Maybe we should talk about whatever is bothering you?"

Ted wasn't listening. He swung his sword and Altalune had no choice but to block him. They kept going like that back and forth till Ted knocked her sword from her hand. Ted stared at it after it hit the ground then looked around him. Whatever was making him angry seemed to be gone because he crumbled from exhaustion and just sat there.

"She cheated on me..." Ted finally said.

"Eleanor?" Altalune asked. "She's many many things but a cheater?"

"She was out with her friend. She brought him to the palace. I had to hear about it from one of the maids. When I confronted her, she couldn't even lie about it because he was lying right there. It was one of the other princes."

"I'm sorry Ted." Altalune sat with him as he let out a heavy sigh.

"Can I come with you guys?" he asked. "As in come on the mission?"

"Sure. We might need your diplomatic status anyway so it wouldn't hurt us if you came along."

"Thanks. I'm going to need time away from her."

"Come on," Altalune said, helping him up. "Let's all have lunch together."

Ted nodded and they all left to have lunch.

The night before they leave for the mission. Altalune was getting ready for bed. She was in her nightgown, her nightly routine done. Feeding Sapphire and Aella was done. Now she was standing at her window talking to Aella and her unicorn boyfriend when there was a knock on the door.

"Gotta go. See you guys in the morning," she said then opened her bedroom door. Finding Eleanor.

"Please let me come on the quest with you!" Eleanor begged.

Altalune sighed and walked to her bed. "No," she said as she sat down.

"Why not?"

"Because you have no reason for coming."

"Neither does Ted and I desperately need to talk to him!"

"Ted is a prince. That might give us a little wiggle room when we enter different cities and talk to other royals. He also wants to get away from you."

"Then take me instead of Calla or Damon."

"Calla's magic could come in handy. Damon knows his way around the underworld, and since our first stop is Daimonas, the city of Demons, which is on the other side of the Tartarus pit, we need him."

"Please, please take me with you!" Eleanor begged even more.

"Look. It's late I need sleep and Ted made it clear he needs time away from you. So you can either try to talk to him before we leave or wait until we come back." Altalune laid down and covered up with the blanket.

"But you coming back could take forever. I need his forgiveness now!"

"Maybe you should have thought about that before you brought another guy to Ted's palace. Now please let me get some sleep."

"He's just a friend, he needed a place to crash Please!"

"If I promise to at least talk to him, will you get out of my house?"

"Yes."

"Fine. I'll talk to him when I feel he's ready to talk."

"Thank you so much!" Eleanor hugged her and left the room.

Altalune groaned in annoyance before going to sleep. In the morning Altalune, Damon and Calla are just about ready to go.

"Mom stop, I'm fine," Altalune said as she brushed her mom's hands away from adding more things in her bag.

"But sweetheart it's still freezing if you don't take an extra jacket, you won't have one in case your first one gets destroyed," her mom complained.

"Mom, if you put any more things in my bag, it'll be too heavy."

"It's ok, Miss Astra. I got this," Calla said and held her hands towards her friends. Her hands started glowing a soft red of magic aura. Then as she closes her eyes the aura surrounds Altalune, Damon, Ted, and herself.

"Woah I'm starting to warm up," Ted said, looking at his hands.

"Me too," Damon said.

"Hey, don't warm me too much. I actually like being cold," Altalune said.

"Ok Ok." Calla does she was asked. "There all done."

"Thanks," Altalune said.

"You're welcome." They hugged.

"Wait! Don't go yet!" They all looked and saw Lucas running over.

"Hey Lucas. Is everything ok?"

He stopped to catch his breath. "Yeah, I just forgot to give you this." He handed her something wrapped in cloth. Altalune took it and unwrapped it.

"It's a sword."

"It's a sword specially designed for you. I was scared it wouldn't be finished before you left. Guess we got lucky."

Altalune examined it. It was simple but beautiful with a single sapphire shimmering in the middle of the hilt.

"Awesome. Thanks Lucas. Oh remember to keep an eye on Asterius. Make sure he's keeping up with his studies and training." She took a folded piece of paper from her back pocket. "This is a list of dos and don'ts as well as a list of things that calm him down when he's upset. Be extra careful when he's raging, he's already broken three desks."

"Why me?" he asked, confused with a hint of fear.

"Because you're my big brother that's why."

"But wouldn't you trust Ted more?"

"She probably would, except I'm coming with her," Ted said.

"It doesn't matter, we need to get going. Dad's waiting," Damon said.

"We are actually going to meet the god Hades!" Calla said with excitement.

"We saw him at the meadow," Altalune said before whistling. Sapphire flew from one of the trees and landed on her shoulder.

"I know but it's still exciting," Calla said

"Stay safe please," Altalune's mom said as they walked away.

Chapter 20

"Tell me again why we are walking to find that unicorn instead of you summoning it to us?" Damon asked.

"That unicorn has a name. I named him Tynan and just because I can understand and speak to horses, Unicorn etc. doesn't mean they have to be at my beckon call," Altalune said.

"I'm just saying. It would make things a whole lot easier on us," Damon said.

"So would getting to the underworld the same way you do," Ted said.

"I can't carry all four of us; it'll drain almost all my energy," Damon argued.

"That's why we are going to find Tynan. He can open a portal that will take us there with ease," Altalune said.

"Hey, can I make a small request? I want to visit my guild and tell the master what's going on?" Calla asked.

"Master Marco." Altalune thought about it. Then nodded. "Sure I don't mind. I have a few questions. For him myself. Are you boys ok with a little detour?"

"Yeah sure," Ted said.

"Fine, let's go," Damon said.

It took two days for them to get back to the town. They went back to the Rainbow phoenix guild. The boys sat down and ordered some lunch while Calla and Altalune went to the back room. Marco was sitting at his desk doing paperwork when they walked in. He had blond hair and pale skin.

"Good afternoon, Master," Calla said. Marco looked up and Altalune noticed his eyes were as blue as the sky. He looked at Calla. Then Altalune and his eyes widened.

"Is something wrong?" Altalune asked, confused.

Marco stood up immediately. "A blue phoenix!" He walked around his desk and walked to Altalune. He held out his hand.

Sapphire hopped onto it, chirping happily as she fluttered her wings a little. "It's been such a long time since I've seen one. He's so young."

"She. I think," Altalune said. "Her name is Sapphire."

"I've never seen one so young before. Her feathers sparkle like an adults," Marco said, gently lifting her left wing.

"That's because she likes eating gems and metals but her favorites are any blue gems, diamonds and silver or white gold," Altalune said.

Marco walked back behind the desk he held sapphire close to the bird tree he had in the corner. Sapphire jumped onto it then Marco crouched to the floor. Calla and Altalune couldn't see what he was doing but before long he stood up again. He unlocked a small treasure box and opened it revealing what was inside.

Altalune gasped. "Blue diamonds!"

"They are extremely rare. Only found in the mountains closest to the vampire city. The last phoenix I saw led me there. I didn't go into the city itself but there were more blue diamonds than I could have ever imagined." Marco took one from the chest and held it up for Sapphire. She looked at the gem then hopped a little closer. She pecked at it till it broke then started eating the smaller pieces.

Her feathers start to shimmer and sparkle even more. Once done she cooed and hopped on the lid of the chest and pecked at more diamonds. "Uh-uh," Marco said and took her off the lid and closed it. "Save the rest for later." Marco walked back to Altalune letting Sapphire hop back onto her shoulder. Then gave her the chest. "Here. Give them to her as a treat. It's better than them collecting dust in my office."

"Thank you, sir," Altalune said and put the chest in her bag.

"Now what is it that you needed?" Marco asked.

"I'm going on another mission with Altalune and some friends. I have no idea how long I'm going to be gone but I hope traveling with them will allow me to learn a lot more magic," Calla said.

"I'm sure it will. Thank you for letting me know. All I ask is that you write to me telling me about your progress and adventures along the way," Marco said.

Calla grinned. "Of course I will."

"And remember, magic isn't some kind of miraculous power. It is a talent that only works when the flow of energy inside of us and the flow of energy in the natural world are in perfect sync. It takes a strong mind and the ability to focus and when you have that the magic should come pouring out of your soul," Marco said. "As long as you have focus and you believe in yourself. You should have no problem learning all the different kinds of magic you want."

"Thanks master!" Calla hugged him and ran out to meet the boys.

Marco looked at Altalune. "Is there something you need?"

"Um." Altalune slowly sat in a chair. "I was wondering if you could tell me something."

"That depends on what you want to know." Marco sat down in his chair.

Altalune opened one of the smaller pockets of her bag and handed him a folded piece of paper. "Do you know who this is?"

Marco unfolded the paper and studied the content. "This looks like Marilla Astra. She was a very very powerful wizard."

"Astra? That's my last name," Altalune said in shock.

Marco looked up at her and set the paper down. "I see the resemblance."

"I-I think I'm her granddaughter but when I saw her in my dreams, she looked so young?" Altalune asked.

"That is most likely because she was still relatively young when she disappeared."

"She disappeared? How?"

"No one knows."

Altalune looked at the drawing she did of her grandmother. "Do you know why me and my mom don't have magic? Especially since Marilla was so powerful?"

"Not everyone can use magic. Like I said to Calla, magic calls for a strong mind and the ability to focus as well as the energy in us and the energy in the natural world are in sync."

"I have no idea whether or not my energy is in sync with the natural world but I know for a fact I have very little focus."

"Then there's your answer."

Altalune sighed softly and stood up. "Thank you for your help. Sir."

"No problem."

Altalune left the office and found her way back to her friends. "Hey guys,"

"Hey Lun. I ordered you a salad," Ted said.

"Thanks," she said and sat next to him.

As they ate Altalune remained silent while her friends talked about the things that could happen on their quest. Once they finished. They went back to finding Tynan. They found him with his herd. Which was a mix of Unicorn Pegasus and Alicorns.

"Alicorns," Ted said in awe. "I had no idea those actually existed."

"Stay here," Altalune said calmly. "Most of these guys aren't used to humans. So they'll be scared if too many of us approach at once. They are already getting agitated."

"Alright we'll leave you to it," Damon said.

"But I want to pet the horses," Calla whined.

Altalune walked over to the herd. "Good afternoon."

"Welcome to the herd," Aella said softly. They hugged each other.

"Tynan," Altalune said as she curtsied and Tynan bowed his head. "Would you please help us. We need to get to the underworld but Damon isn't strong enough to take all four of us without passing out."

"Yes. I remember," Tynan said in her head. His horn growled in a dark bluish purple aura like before then a few feet away a shimmering portal in the same color of his aura appeared.

"Thank you so much I'll repay you later," Altalune said.

"There will be no need for that," Tynan told her. "Good luck on your mission, you'll need it."

"Thank you. Let's go, you guys." Altalune led the way, through the portal her friends close behind. Once through the other side. They were standing outside the gates of Hades palace.

"Next stop. Daimonas city," Damon said.

www.ingramcontent.com/pod-product-compliance
Lightning Source LLC
LaVergne TN
LVHW041220080526
838199LV00082B/1342